A laugh in the dark.

It was then that we heard the burst of wicked laughter behind us. The hair on my back and neck stood straight up.

"Drover, was that you laughing?"

"N-n-no."

"And it wasn't me. Do you see what this means?"

Then came the eerie voice from the darkness. "Hi, fellas. Out for a little stroll? I guess you thought I was gone, huh? Well, darn the luck. I came back."

"Drover, we have a problem. And I hear water running."

"It's me. I want to go home!"

"Back to the porch, son. Go to Turbo Five and don't speak to any strangers. Let's hit it!"

I went to Full Flames and Turbo five on all engines and . . . BONK! . . . ran into something big and hairy. I bounced off it and went streaking through the darkness and didn't slow down until I had made it to the safety of the front porch.

The Case of the Raging Rottweiler

The Case of the
Raging Rottweiler

John R. Erickson

Illustrations by Gerald L. Holmes

Viking

VIKING
Published by the Penguin Group
Penguin Putnam Books for Young Readers,
345 Hudson Street, New York, New York 10014, U.S.A.
Penguin Books Ltd, 27 Wrights Lane, London W8 5TZ, England
Penguin Books Australia Ltd, Ringwood, Victoria, Australia
Penguin Books Canada Ltd, 10 Alcorn Avenue,
Toronto, Ontario, Canada M4V 3B2
Penguin Books (N.Z.) Ltd, 182-190 Wairau Road, Auckland 10, New Zealand

Penguin Books Ltd, Registered Offices: Harmondsworth, Middlesex, England

Published simultaneously by Viking and Puffin Books, divisions
of Penguin Putnam Books for Young Readers, 2000

1 3 5 7 9 10 8 6 4 2

LIBRARY OF CONGRSS CATALOGING-IN-PUBLICATION DATA
Erickson, John R., date
The case of the raging Rottweiler / John R. Erickson ;
illustrations by Gerald L. Holmes.
p. cm. — (Hank the Cowdog ; 36)
Summary: A huge Rottweiler the size of King Kong (according to Hank)
threatens the security of Hank the Cowdog's ranch.
ISBN 0-670-89364-1 — ISBN 0-14-130668-8 (pbk.)
1. Dogs—Fiction 2. Rottweiler dog—Fiction. 3. Ranch life—West (U.S.)—Fiction.
4. West (U.S.)—Fiction. 5. Humorous stories.]
I. Holmes, Gerald L., ill. II. Title.
PZ7.E72556 Caq 2000 [Fic]—dc21 00-029091

Hank the Cowdog® is a registered trademark of John R. Erickson.

Printed in the U.S.A
Set in New Century Schoolbook

To the memory of Lane Anderson

CONTENTS

CHAPTER ONE

The Mystery Begins

It's me again, Hank the Cowdog. The mystery began one evening toward the end of May, as I recall. Yes, it was May. I'm sure it was, because "May" is a three-letter word that if spelled backward comes out "yam." A yam is a sweet potato, don't you see, and is similar to a regular Irish potato.

What does all this have to do with the Case of the Raging Rottweiler? Be patient, I'm getting there.

See, in the Security Business, we often employ little memory tricks to help us recall the many facts and clues we encounter in our work. Example: "May" spelled backward comes out "yam." A yam is a form of potato, right? You will be shocked to know that the night this adventure began, Slim cooked himself *a baked potato* for supper.

1

You see the connection now? It all fits together—
May, yam, Irish potato, and baked potato—and
that's how I remember that this case began in May.
Pretty clever, huh? You bet. In the Security Business, we often employ . . . I've already said that.

Where were we? We were at the beginning, and
that happens to be the point at which most of these
mysteries begin. It all began, as I recall, around the
middle of June. We were in the grip of a heat wave,
day after day of temperatures over a hundred
degrees. Terrible heat, and also very dry.

No rain. Our spring grass had turned brown.
The buffalo grass had stopped growing. Stock ponds
were drying up and turning into mudholes. Slim
was keeping a close watch on our windmills, checking them every other day instead of the usual twice
a week.

Have we discussed the importance of windmills
on a cattle ranch? Maybe not, but I guess we should.
On a ranching operation such as this one, most of
our water for the livestock is pumped out of the
ground by windmills. Nothing is more important in
the summertime than a supply of fresh water. If cattle run out of water, fellers, we have big problems.
We either have to haul water to the cattle in a
water trailer or move the cattle to another pasture.

What makes the water situation especially

scary is that if the wind quits blowing, the windmills quit turning—all of them. And then we have water problems everywhere at once. Our situation wasn't quite that serious. It was hot and dry, but the wind was still blowing and turning those windmills, and for that we were grateful.

It's kind of impressive that a dog would know so much about ranch management, isn't it? Most of your ordinary mutts (Drover comes to mind here) pay no attention to such matters. They eat, lie around in the shade, scratch a few fleas, and maybe bark at a cat every once in a while, but they pay no attention to the Larger Issues.

Me? I have to stay on top of things. Have I mentioned that I'm Head of Ranch Security? I am, which means I'm not only in charge of Surveillance and Investigations, but I have to keep a close eye on these other matters, too.

Anyways, it was July and hot. Drover and I had spent the day checking cattle and windmills with Slim Chance, the cowboy. It was around eight o'clock in the evening, just before sundown, when we returned to Slim's shack, some two miles east of ranch headquarters. Slim got out of the pickup and stretched a kink out of his back. Whilst he was involved in that, Drover and I left our spots on the pickup seat and jumped out.

3

I noticed that a scowl moved across Slim's face and that his eyes seemed to have locked on . . . something, something inside the pickup. The seat perhaps? It was hard to tell, but Slim was giving it a close inspection.

"Is there some reason why you mutts have to shed hair all over my pickup seat?"

Well, I . . . I didn't know how to respond to that. Had we shed a few hairs?

He pointed toward the evidence. "Look at that. I let you bozos ride up front with the executives, and that's the thanks I get."

I looked closer. You know, he was right. Even at a distance, I could see that certain unnamed suspects had deposited ugly dog hairs on the back of his pickup seat.

I whirled around and stabbed Drover with a glare of steel. "You see what you've done?"

He blinked his eyes and grinned. "Oh, hi. Are we home already? Gosh, I must have dozed off."

"Of course you dozed off. You always doze off, but that's not the problem."

"Oh good. I sure love sleep. What's the problem?"

I pointed my nose toward the inside of the pickup. "Check that out, Drover. Study the evidence."

4

He studied the evidence. "Well, let's see here. I don't see anything."

"Dog hairs. Hundreds of 'em, thousands of 'em. They're all over Slim's pickup seat. Can you guess where they came from?"

He sat down and squinted one eye. "Well, let me think. Uh . . . a dog?"

"Very good. Cat hair comes from cats. Hog hair comes from hogs. Dog hair comes from dogs."

"I'll be derned. I didn't know hogs had hair."

"They do. All fur-boring animals have hair. Hogs are boring animals. Therefore, they have hair."

"I thought they had bristles."

"No. You're thinking of brushes. Brushes have bristles. Hogs have hair."

"I'll be derned. What makes 'em so boring?"

"They're boring, Drover, because they grunt all the time. If they had anything to say, maybe they wouldn't be so boring, but their answer to everything is a grunt."

"Yeah, and who cares what a hog thinks anyway?"

"Exactly my point. And let that be a lesson to you."

Just then, Slim pointed down to the creek. "Lookie yonder. There's our doe and fawn again."

He gave us the evil eye. "Don't you dogs even *think* about chasing those deer."

Who, me? Hey, he didn't need to . . .

Sure enough, on the other side of the creek was a whitetail doe and her fawn. They'd been coming in for water the past several days, and Slim sure didn't need to worry about me barking them away. No sir. The thought had never . . .

Okay, maybe I'd thought about it once or twice. I mean, barking at wild animals was second nature to a dog, but Slim had made his position clear on the matter and I had taken a solemn pledge not to bother his deer. Heck, I had even promised to protect them.

At that very moment, my ears picked up the sound of an approaching vehicle. That was odd, very odd. Who would be coming to Slim's place at this hour of the day? I didn't know, and it didn't really matter. The vehicle had no business on our ranch, and it was time for us dogs to bark the alarm.

"Drover, we've got an unidentified vehicle coming in from the south. This could turn into a Code Three Situation. Let's move out."

We went streaking past Slim's pitiful little yard. It was pitiful because it contained no grass, only weeds, and most of those weeds were withered and brown from the heat. We roared past the yard, past the house, and went ripping up the hill to the cattle guard.

There, sure enough, we met the Unauthorized Vehicle. Description: old Ford, faded blue, conventional box bed, a dent in the right fender. A driver appeared to be sitting . . . well, in the driver's seat. I guess that wasn't such a big clue, but I took note of it anyway.

When you're Head of Ranch Security, you have to notice every tiny detail. I mean, if there had been no driver, that would have been . . . never mind.

But there was a driver. A man, age . . . I couldn't tell his age. Maybe forty. He was wearing a straw cowboy hat and a T-shirt, an odd combination. See, cowboys—your real working cowboys—wear *long-sleeved* shirts, never T-shirts. There are reasons for that, but we're in the middle of a Code Three and I don't have time to go into them now.

Oh, maybe we can pause for just a minute. Cowboys wear long-sleeved shirts to protect themselves from sun and biting insects. Men who wear T-shirts usually aren't ranch cowboys.

Okay, back to the Unidentified Vehicle. We swooped in on it, Drover and I did, and within seconds we had it surrounded. I gave the order to initiate Warning Barks. When the pickup didn't screech to a halt, we shifted into the next stage, which we call "You'd Better Stop That Thing Right Now."

It's a more serious kind of barking, don't you see, and a lot of times the driver of the vehicle will slam on his brakes and step out of the cab with his hands in the air. No kidding.

But that's not what this guy did. He kept driving, I mean, just ignored us, kept going and left us in a cloud of dust. Caliche dust, very fine and powdery because of the dryness of the weather, and I didn't appreciate having to breathe it.

Already I wasn't liking this guy, and then I noticed a couple of clues that made me like him even less. First off, he had two fishing poles hanging out the window on the passenger side, an indication that he might be a poached fisherman.

A fishing poacherman.

A poaching fisherman.

A poacher. A trespasser. The kind of guy who slips onto a ranch and fishes without the permission of the owners. I don't like 'em. They have no respect for private property. They come in without permission, catch fish, and leave their garbage behind—candy wrappers, beer cans, soda pop bottles—and we have to clean up the mess.

So, right away, I had three or four good rea-

sons for disliking this guy, and after choking on his dust for a few seconds, I sprang back into action and chased him all the way to Slim's little shack of a barn. Drover fell in behind me and added a few yips.

It must have worked. The trespasser pulled up beside Slim's pickup and stopped. I quit barking and waited to see what would happen.

Slim slouched against the pickup and stuck out his hand. "Well I'll be derned. Joe McCall. I haven't seen you in a while."

They shook hands. "It was at a team roping in Higgins, wasn't it?"

"That's right. Me and Loper were lookin' at the prize money right up to the last go-round. Then you caught your steer in seven seconds flat. We went home broke, and I've been broke ever since. I always figured it was mostly your fault."

Joe laughed. "We got lucky, is all. You guys were hot that night. You still rope?"

"In the pasture, is all. My banker sent a little note with my fifth overdraft and said I might want to explore other career opportunities. I guess he'd done figured out that I wasn't going to make it to the National Finals."

Joe nodded and smiled. "I hear you. Me too. Having to grow up is terrible, ain't it?"

"I wouldn't know. I'm still fightin' it. Well, heck, get out and stretch your legs. What brings you out here to the wilderness?"

Joe got out and stretched. "Well, I had a day off and did a little fishing at the lake. I was on my way home and thought I'd stop by and say howdy."

Slim's gaze went to the bed of the pickup. "What's that you're hauling back there?"

Joe's smile faded. "Oh, that's Bruiser, my brother's dog. He's a rottweiler. I'm baby-sitting this week."

I shot a glance at Drover. "Did you hear that? There's an unauthorized dog in the back of that pickup. Come on, son, we need to check this out."

We went streaking over to the pickup, and so the mystery began.

Bruiser, the Raging Rottweiler

Joe let down the tailgate of the pickup, just as Drover and I arrived to begin our investigation of this new dog.

Have we discussed the ranch's position on visiting dogs? Maybe not. We always check 'em out pretty carefully, and for very good reason. Some of those town dogs will try to chase cattle, and that's a major No-No. A huge No-No. In ranch country, dogs who chase cattle are very unpopular, and they don't last long.

Yes, we would have to speak with this mutt and get a few things . . .

HUH?

I saw him. There he was.

That wasn't a dog. It was a BEAR, a huge, enormous grizzly bear!

I, uh, did a sudden about-face and found my steps leading to the underside of Joe's, uh, pickup, so to speak. There, to my surprise, I found Drover cowering in the dust.

"What are you doing under here? You're supposed to be interrogating that dog."

"Not me. I saw him, and he looks like a gorilla. I never interrogate gorillas."

"Oh, rubbish. He's just a dog. He puts on his pants the same way we do."

"His pants would make a tent for me. You go. I'll wait here."

Well, I couldn't allow Drover to know . . . to think, let us say, that I was . . . well . . . nervous or uneasy about this new dog on the ranch. I mean, that would have ruined him—Drover, that is. Part of my job on this outfit is setting a good example for all the employees of the Security Division. For Drover, actually. Someone from the Security Division had to check it out, and it appeared that it would be me.

I gave the runt a withering glare. "All right, I'll go, but I must warn you, Drover. This will have to go into my report."

"Fine with me."

"What?"

"I said . . . oh darn. Drat."

"I'm sorry, but the regulations are very clear on this. You will get three Chicken Marks."

With that, I whirled away from Drover and marched . . . okay, maybe I didn't march out from under the pickup. I scooted and crawled, but the important thing was that I put in an appearance. I was there to show the flag for the Security Division, and to let this mutt know . . .

He saw me and started growling.

. . . to let this fella know how happy we were to, uh, have visitors on the ranch. We don't get many visitors, don't you know, and it was always nice . . .

I worked up a friendly smile and waved a paw in greeting. "Hi there."

He glared and growled. Gad, what an ugly dog! What had they called him? A "rottenwiler"? He looked rotten, all right, rotten and enormous. I mean, the guy must have weighed a hundred pounds.

A rottweiler, that's what they called him.

Anyways, we were sure proud to have him visiting the ranch. I sat very still and listened.

Joe sat on the tailgate and called the dog to him. "Come here, Bruiser. Be still. Those dogs won't hurt you."

Slim took a toothpick out of his hatband and ran it through his teeth. "That's a mighty big dog. I'd say there ain't much chance that Hank and Drover would hurt him. I've heard stories about them rottweilers. Some of 'em have a bad attitude."

Joe nodded. "He is a big dog, and he ought to be able to whip his weight in wildcats. But you know, he's as silly as a goose. Most of the time he goes around acting like King Kong, but he's scared to death of my wife's cat."

"Aw heck. Scared of a cat?"

"Yes sir. And the other day, he saw himself in a mirror and spent three hours hiding in the closet. To tell you the truth, I think he's a little bit . . ." Joe's finger drew circles in the air beside his head. "I'll be glad when my brother gets back home."

Just then, Bruiser's head shot up. He'd seen our doe and fawn down by the creek. A growl sprang from his throat. He started barking and made a lunge. Joe grabbed one of his legs and tried to hang on, but Bruiser tore away from him, dived out of the pickup, and headed straight for the deer.

"Bruiser, come back here! Bruiser!"

Well, I was just sitting there, observing and minding my own business. Next thing I knew, Slim was standing over me. "Hank, go get 'im. Stop that dog before he kills the fawn."

I stared into his face. *What?* Stop the dog? Was he crazy? That dog, for his information, gave every appearance of being a hundred-and-fifty-pound wrecking machine, and if Slim thought . . .

He grabbed my tail and hoisted me up. "I hate to ask you to do this, but I'm asking. Get him stopped and I'll be right behind you. Now go!"

I swallowed a lump in my throat and looked toward the creek. Well, if Bruiser was afraid of cats, maybe . . .

When the mother deer saw that big lunk of a dog heading her way, she flashed her white tail and sprinted off to the east. That was the good part. The bad part was that the fawn tried to follow but tripped over some weeds. He was pretty young, see, and had spindly legs, and he fell down.

Bruiser was headed straight for him. Oh, did I mention that Bruiser ran like a fat duck? No kidding, he did. He couldn't run worth a dern.

He plowed through the shallow water, leaped up on the east bank of the creek, and lunged right at the fawn and pinned it with his massive paws.

Gulp. Well, it was clear what I had to do. I didn't want to, but when you're Head of Ranch Security, you answer the calls and hope for the . . . gulp . . . best.

I hit Sirens and Lights and went straight into

a Code Three. The second one of the day, in case you're counting. Using my incredible speed, I was able to close the distance between myself and the rottweiler. I roared up to the crime scene and went right to work.

"Halt in the name of the law! Come out with your hands up. You're under arrest!"

Standing over the fawn, Bruiser heard my command and turned his ugly eyes on me. "What did you say?"

I tried to hide the quivering of my voice. "I said, why don't you pick on someone your own size?"

He lumbered over to me. That wasn't such great news, but it allowed the fawn to jump up and run away. Bruiser glared at me. "My own size? How about you?"

"Me? Well, I . . . you're quite a bit bigger than me, actually, and I'm sure you'll agree . . ."

"Shut up, moron. You messed up my fun, and now I'm fixing to . . ."

"Bruiser! Bruiser! Down, boy."

Whew! The men arrived just in time. Joe clipped a chain around Bruiser's neck and pulled him off before he was able to get me skinned and gutted.

Joe was panting for breath. "Sorry about that, Slim. I never thought about him chasing deer. Boy, he's stout, ain't he?"

"Uh-huh, and I'm thinking he just had one of his King Kong moments." Slim came over to me, knelt down, and took my head in his hands. "How you doing, pardner?"

Still in one piece—barely.

"Nice work, pooch. You probably saved my fawn, so I guess that makes you a hero—as incredible as that may seem."

No kidding? Me, a hero? Gee, from where I was watching, it hadn't seemed all that great. I mean, let's face it: the dog had been one step away from trashing me. But if Slim insisted that I was a hero . . . well, maybe I was.

I held my head at a proud angle and listened to the cheers of the crowd. A marching band was playing—drums and fifes and blaring trumpets. Lady dogs from all over Texas pushed their way to the front and tossed flowers in my direction.

And there, in front of the whole multitude, Sally May fought her way through the crowd, and when her gaze fell upon my battered body, a cry of anguish leapt from her anguished throat, and in an anguished voice, she cried, "Oh, Hank, my beloved Hank, what hath they done to you?" And then she ungulfed me in the embrace of her loving arms and—you won't believe this part—she kissed me on the cheek.

Pretty swell, huh?

With the cheers of the crowd still ringing in my ears, I gave myself a good shake and saw . . . Drover.

"Oh my gosh, Hank, what happened?"

"I gave the bully a sound thrashing. What did you expect?"

His eyes grew as wide as plates. "No fooling? Gosh, I never thought . . ."

"I only wish the men had given me another

minute. One more minute and I would have whipped the stuffings out of the big lug."

The men had started back toward the pickups, leading the beaten, humiliated rottenweiler. Drover and I fell in behind them.

"You mean, you really whipped him? You're not just making it up?"

"How many times should I say it, Drover? Yes, yes, and yes. I'm shocked that you show so little confidence in my combat techniques."

"Yeah, but he's so big . . ."

I gave a careless chuckle. "Son, never forget that it isn't the size of the dog in the fight that matters. It's the size of the fog in the dog. He's big, Drover, but also slow and dumb, very dumb. Oh, and we happen to know that he's scared of cats."

The pitiful, beaten, humiliated Bruiser heard this. His head shot up and he glared back at me. "What did you just say?"

Drover let out a gasp. "Hank, shhh, he's listening."

"Relax, son, I'll handle this." I raised my voice so that the little wimp of a rottweiler could hear. "I said you're slow and dumb. I said you're nothing but a scaredy cat who's scared of cats. I said you walk like a fat duck. What do you think of that?"

He lunged against the chain and exposed a

mouthful of . . . my goodness, for a spineless little weenie, he had some huge teeth. "Why, I oughta break your neck!"

I gave him a pleasant smile. "Yes, but you had your chance and you didn't get it done. Do you know why? Because . . ."

Drover was about to have a stroke. "Hank, shhhhh!"

"Because you fight like a fat duck. Oh, you're pretty tough when it comes to beating up baby deer, but put you in the ring with the Head of Ranch Security and you stink."

He lunged at me again, and this time I could feel his hot breath on my face. I ignored him and went right on. "In fact, you stink twice—once for fighting like a fat duck and once for your breath, which smells like garbage."

Drover was moaning and rolling his eyes. "Hank, don't do this!"

Bruiser's eyes were flaming now. "Listen, stupid, if I ever get off this chain, I'm gonna finish what I started."

"Oh yeah? Well, bring a sack lunch, fatso, 'cause it's liable to take you a couple of days. See you around, and don't ever set foot on my ranch again."

Joe and Mister Big Talker got into the cab of the pickup and drove off. As they pulled away from the house, Bruiser was glaring at me with eyes filled with meanness and hatred.

I turned to Drover. "Well, one riot, one cowdog. Too bad you were hiding under the pickup. You missed all the fun."

He was shaking his head and rolling his eyes. "I don't think you should have said all those things."

"Why? Hey, it served him right, and besides, we'll never see him again."

Those turned out to be famous last words.

Slim Clips
His Toenails

Slim watched them until the pickup left our property and turned right on the county road. Then he looked down at me.

"Boys, that right there is a bad dog. Joe's going to have problems with him. Nice work, Hank." He bent down and scratched me behind the ears. I puffed myself up to my full height and shot a grin at Mister Squeakbox. "You ain't much of a fighter, but your heart's in the right place. I'll remember that the next time you mess up."

Huh?

There! You see what these guys do? They give you a little compliment, a little pat on the head, and then they take it all back with some tacky remark. *I'll remember that the next time you mess up.* What an insult. What an outrage!

For his information, I rarely ever "mess up," and I had no plans for "messing up" any time in the near future.

I couldn't believe he'd said that. Oh well.

Where were we? Oh yes, at the end of a long hot day in August. Bushed. Beat. Exhausted. Worn down to a nub of our former selves but triumphant, since I had won a huge moral victory over an overbearing rottweiler. And we had ended our long, hot so forth down at Slim's bachelor shack, on the banks of Wolf Creek.

We dogs kind of enjoyed staying down at Slim's place. For one thing, he, being a bachelor, had no problem with dogs staying inside his house. Not that we were dirty, understand. We weren't—or I wasn't. I can't speak for Drover or speculate on his personal habits relating to cleanliness, but I can certainly speak for myself.

I'm pretty derned fussy about my appearance. I bathe every single day in the overflow of the septic tank. It not only leaves me clean and spotless, but it also gives me that deep, manly aroma that the lady dogs really love.

Where were we? Oh yes. Slim always let us stay inside the house, and once there, we often found ourselves in position to . . . how can I say this? Once we established a presence inside the house, we were then in a perfect and natural position to . . . well, share in his meals. Snack. Eat. He sometimes gave us food, is the point, and food is a very important part of a dog's . . . whatever.

Spiritual development, I suppose. Feeling of well-bean. See, even on a bad day, a few morsels of food can bring a flood of new meaning into our lives.

We ask so little of this life, we dogs, and a few scraps of food can turn a slow day into an exciting experience. For all his flots and falls . . . for all his flaws and flots . . . for all his faults and flaws, let us say, old Slim often scored home runs in the Sharing of Food Department.

Anyways, Drover and I made our way up to the house. Slim had gotten there first and was inside doing . . . something. Taking off his boots, perhaps. Yes, that's exactly what he was doing. I knew, because I heard him straining with the boot jack, and then I heard his boots hit the floor.

Bam. Bam. Two boots. That's what he wore, two boots, because . . . well, he had two feet, I suppose, and if a guy has two feet, he wears . . . skip it.

We made our way up to the front porch and went to the screen door. A lot of your common run of ranch mutts—and we're talking about mutts with no class or couth or manners—would start scratching on the screen door. Not me. I knew better than to do such a thing. Not only was it discouthful and rude, but that door-scratching had a tendency to ... well, destroy screens.

I knew Slim's position on Damaged Screen Doors. He didn't approve. They made him mad and caused him to roar and yell. Hencely, instead of scratching on the door, I sat down on the porch and positioned myself so that he could see me.

Drover was there, too, and together we sat down and waited for Slim to let us in. Minutes passed. We could hear him in there. He was doing ... something.

Click. Click. Click.

My ears leaped up and I twisted my head to the side as I tried to analyze the sound. "What's he doing in there?"

"Well, I don't know, but it sounds kind of like ... you don't reckon he's clipping his toenails, do you?"

I gave the runt a glare. "Clipping his toenails? Don't be ridiculous. Why would he clip his toenails at a time like this?"

"Well, I don't know. What time is it?"

"It's time for us to be off duty and inside the house, where we belong. Besides, Slim would never go to the trouble of clipping his toenails. He just tears them off."

"Oh, okay."

Click. Click. Click.

"Drover, unless I'm badly mistaken, he's in there clipping his toenails."

"I'll be derned. I never would have thought of that."

"Nor would I, but the evidence is building up. That clicking sound, you see, is coming from the toenail clipper as it clips each of the various toenails."

"I'll swan."

"And obviously he doesn't realize that we're out here, waiting to be let in." I paused a moment to ponder the situation. "Okay, Drover, let's go into Loyal Dogs Waiting Patiently. Do you remember the routine?"

"Well, let me think. We sit and . . . stare at the door?"

"Almost. We sit and stare at the door and sweep our tails across the porch."

"Yeah, but my tail's just a stub and it can't sweep."

"Good point. I hadn't thought of that. Okay, I'll switch my tail over to Slow Sweeps, and you wiggle yours. How about that?"

"That'll work. I can do pretty good wiggles."

And that's just what we did, went into Loyal

Dogs Waiting Patiently and did a heck of a job with it. But it didn't work.

Click. Click. Click.

"Hmmm. He seems to be ignoring us."

"Yeah, and I'm getting discouraged."

"Don't give up, son, we've got a few more bags in our trick. Maybe we should sing the 'Let Us in the House' song. That'll get him."

And with that, we belted out the song, just like this.

Let Us in the House Song

There's a time for everything.
There's a time for working.
There's a time for suffering.
And there's a time we should call it quits.

We dogs have worked in heat and dust,
And that's without complaining,
But what's the deal? This door is shut,
And there's some risk that we'll starve
    to death.

Must you clip your toenails?
And must you do it now?
We're sitting on the front porch
Waiting to be let inside.

We don't really want to
Cause you any trouble.
Can't you merely take the hint?
'Cause if you don't we will scratch
   the screen.

Summer heat is hard on us
And these drought conditions.
We've just put in a long, hard day
Protecting you from all kinds of stuff.

We don't want to threaten,
Bark or beg or moan,
But this is getting serious.
Your nails can wait for another time.

Must you clip your toenails?
And must you do it now?
We're sitting on the front porch
Waiting to be let inside.

We don't really want to
Cause you any trouble.
Can't you merely take the hint?
'Cause if you don't we will scratch
   the screen.

Pretty awesome song, huh? You bet. And I was pretty sure it would do the trick. I cocked my ear and listened.

Click. Click. Click.

"Drover, something's wrong. Surely, if he'd heard our song, he would rush to the door and let us in."

"Maybe he doesn't like us anymore. Maybe he hates us. Remember all those dog hairs on the pickup seat?"

"Those were hog hairs. You told me so yourself."

"I think they were dog hairs, and I think they might have come from . . . us."

"Hmmm. You could be right."

I cut my eyes from side to side and plunged into deep thoughts of deepest concentration. "Okay, what's done is done. There's no use spilling any more milk. If Slim insists on clipping his toenails, we have no choice but to scratch on the screen door."

Drover's eyes widened. "Oh, I don't think we'd better do that. He might get mad."

"Well, it's his own fault. He's brought this upon himself. We tried the course of manners and reason and it flopped."

"I guess we could just stay out on the porch."

I stared at him. "I can't believe you said that.

Stay out on the porch? When there's a whole house waiting for a couple of tired, loyal dogs to come in? What good is a house without dogs, Drover?"

"Well . . . "

"A house without dogs is like a song without a melody, a tree without leaves, a sandwich without mustard, a ranch without baling wire. A house without dogs is a hollow place, just four roofs and a wall."

"And toenail clippers."

"Exactly. A house without dogs is like toenail clippers without a toe. Do you see what this means? It means that we must go to the drastic measure of scratching on the screen."

He gulped. "Which one of us?"

"Me, of course, unless . . . I guess we could let you, uh, go solo on this deal. Yes, it might be good experience for you."

"Yeah, but this old leg's acting up on me again."

"Which leg?"

"The one I use for scratching."

"Use your other leg."

"It's starting to hurt too, terrible pain. I just don't think I could stand it."

I gave my head a shake. "Drover, you are such a weenie. What's the big deal? We're doing this for Slim's own good, don't forget that."

Drover stood up and began limping in a circle.

"Okay, skip it, I'll do the scratching. But this will have to go into my report."

"Oh no, not that!"

"Yes, and all your begging and whining won't change a thing. It will go into my report and you will get five Chicken Marks. How does that make you feel?"

"Oh my leg!"

I ignored his noise and marched up to the screen door. I took three deep breaths, limbered up my scratching paw, and prepared to launch myself into Drastic Measures. Maybe that was a mistake.

CHAPTER FOUR

The Big Mouse Safari

R ight away, I went into my Warm-up and Stretch Exercise Program. I limbered up the big Scratchus Muscle in my right shoulder and extended my claws several times. Then and only then did I place my right front paw on the screen door.

I pulled the paw and claws in a downward direction, creating a scratching sound.

The clicking of the toenail clippers stopped. We heard Slim's feet hit the floor. He was coming to the door. I tossed a glance at Drover and gave him a wink.

"You see? There's nothing to it. You could have done it, if you hadn't been such a . . ."

Yikes. He was standing in front of us. Slim was, not Drover. Drover suddenly ducked his head and went slithering over to the woodpile and took cover. That left me all alone to, uh, face the . . . the music, the charges, the whatever might be . . .

Slim didn't look real happy. I could see it in his face. We dogs are very perceptive, you know, and . . . let's go straight to the point. He was mad about something. But what? Surely not my gentle scratching on his screen. I mean, 1 had been very, VERY careful not to leave ugly scratch marks on his, uh, screen.

Actually, it had been more of a *rubbing* action than a scratching action. Honest. I had hardly used my claws at all.

Maybe he had . . . cut off one of his toes. Yes, that was it. He had been trimming his toenails, see, and in a careless moment he had lost concentration and had . . . well, lopped off one of his toes. That would make a guy mad, wouldn't it? Sure it would. If you only had four toes, you couldn't do "This Little Piggy Went to Market."

Well, I guess you could do some of it, but when you came to the "wee, wee, wee" part, you'd be out of toes. That would be lousy. "Wee, wee, wee" is the best part, right? It's the punch line, so to speak, and if you . . .

Slim loomed above me like a huge tree. Through the screen door, his face had a ghostly haze about it, and all at once he resembled a . . . well, a ghost. An angry ghost.

At last he spoke. "You know what happened to the last dog that scratched up my door?"

I . . . uh . . . no. I had no idea. But I hadn't actually *scratched* the door, see. It had been more of a . . .

"I sold him to a dogsled driver for two dollars and fifty cents, and now he's pulling logs in Siberia."

Siberia? Gee, that's a pretty cold place.

"Don't scratch on my door."

Well, sure, yes. I, uh, knew that, but I . . . that is, Drover and I had felt an urgent need to . . .

"You mutts are shedding hair in this heat, and I don't need dog hair all over my house."

No, of course not, but maybe if we concentrated extra hard on . . .

"And furthermore, I just found a tick crawling on the back of my neck."

A tick? We knew nothing about ticks. Honest. He must have gotten it from . . . well, from a chicken. Or from a passing rabbit.

No, he'd gotten it from Bruiser, the fleabag rott-weiler. That was it.

"I can't think of any reason why you dogs need to be in my nice clean house."

Nice clean . . . oh brother! That was the joke of the century. *His house was a mess.* He knew it, I knew it, everybody knew it. The truth of the matter was that most dogs wouldn't have set foot in the place, for fear of being eaten by mice or dying of dust pneumonia. So if he didn't want us in his house, by George, that was fine with me.

We glared at each other through the screen. Then the hinges squeaked and . . . he opened the door? What was the deal? He'd just gone through this long sermon about . . .

"I'll let y'all in for one reason, and one reason only. It ain't because you deserve to come in, 'cause you don't. It's because a house with me in it is so boring, I can't hardly stand it. Now, get in here, and don't be scratching on my screen door."

Yes sir, you bet! No more screen-scratching for me.

I shot through the door before he could change his mind. Drover was right behind me. The little noodle had ventured out of his hiding place in the woodpile—after I had taken all the heat and the tongue-lashings and the snaky looks—and in a flash, he was curled up on the floor.

I didn't hit the floor at once. Instead, I went into the Digging and Fluffing procedure, the aim of which was to soften up the old threadbare carpet on Slim's . . .

"And don't be digging holes in my new carpet."

New carpet? It was old and ugly. But what the heck, it was probably soft enough, so I did three quick turns and flopped down. Gag! It was as hard as a gravel road.

I turned a glare on my nincompoop assistant. "Well, I hope you're happy. I got us into the house, and what did you do? You hid in the woodpile!"

"No, I saw a mouse."

"You did not see a mouse."

"Well, I thought I saw a mouse, but maybe it was a cricket."

"You didn't see a mouse or a cricket. You were fleeing from reality. You were hiding from Life Itself. What kind of dog are you?"

"Well . . . Mom always said we were Heinz 57, but I'm not sure what that means."

"It means that you can find 57 ways of saving your hiney and putting mine in harm's way. It means that you can find 57 ways of dodging responsibility. Are you ashamed of yourself?"

"Well . . . let me think here."

"If you have to think about it, you're not ashamed."

"Okay, I'm ashamed."

"Are you just saying that or do you really mean it?"

"I really mean it, from my heart. I'm so ashamed,

I can hardly stand myself, but I don't know where else to go."

I studied the runt. He seemed sincere about this. "Okay, if you really mean it, we'll let it slide this time. But those five Chicken Marks will have to stay on your record."

"Oh drat."

"Make it six. One more for naughty language."

I hated to pile on the Chicken Marks, but when you're Head of Ranch Security, you have to be firm with the underlings.

Well, after straightening out Drover, I began thinking seriously about turning in for the night. It had been a long, hard day in the broiling heat of summer and I was ready to send up a few Zs. But before I could get that deal started, Slim came walking into the room.

I lifted my head and looked at him. He had stripped down to his boxer shorts, perhaps because of the heat . . . yes, I'm sure it was the heat. Slim wasn't the kind of guy who went around half-naked without a good reason.

The reason was that his house was as hot as an oven. He didn't have an air commissioner, so there he was, half-naked, with his skinny mayonnaise legs sticking out of his boxer shorts.

I guess he didn't mind exposing his legs to us

dogs. Perhaps he knew that we were accustomed to keeping deep dark secrets about our masters, such as how ridiculous they looked running around the house in their undershorts.

Anyways, he came into the living room, and guess what he was carrying in his right hand: a forked stick with . . . what were those things? Long strips of inner tube? And a piece of leather tied to their ends? Hmmm. That was odd.

"Y'all ready to hunt some mice? They're about to take this place over, and by grabs, I've decided to fight back. Made myself a slingshot."

Oh, so that was it. Yes, of course. Forked stick, strips of inner-tube rubber, piece of leather. The pieces of the puzzle began falling into place. By George, we were fixing to go on a big mouse safari! And yes, I was ready to contribute my part to the effort.

I turned to Drover. "Well, this is going to be more exciting than I . . ." He had vanished. Out of the corner of my eye, I saw him slinking down the hall. A moment later, I heard him crawling under Slim's bed. Oh well, we would do better without him.

He's scared of mice, you know. And loud noises.

And so it was that Slim and I opened hunting season on the local mice. Here's how we did it. Slim moved his big stuffed chair into the kitchen, so that he not only had a comfortable seat but also had a good view of the part of his kitchen that contained the most . . . well, mouse bait, I guess you would say.

We're talking about bread crumbs, cracker crumbs, jelly spills, bits of tuna fish, canned mackerel, and Vienna sausage that had ended up on the floor. Slim had studied the behavioral patterns of the local mouse population, don't you see, and had made some important discoveries.

First off, the mice hid out during the daylight hours. Second, they tended to come out and show themselves after dark. Third, when they showed themselves, they went straight into the kitchen, where they began gorging themselves on the various food groups on the floor.

Slim had made note of their feeding patterns and had devised a hunting stragedy. Strategy. He would lounge in the chair until a mouse showed himsclf. At that point, he would load four or five BBs into the slingshot, pull 'er back, and let fly with the buckshot. (He used four or five BBs because he was a lousy shot. We dogs know these secrets about our human friends.)

Pretty slick, huh? You bet it was. And you talk about FUN. Fellers, this promised to be good, wholesome family entertainment, fun with a

41

higher social purpose (ridding the house of nasty mice). I'm sure it would have been loads of fun and there's no telling how many mice we might have gotten if . . .

See, Slim fired off his first shot. He missed the mouse and BBs went flying everywhere. There was a crashing sound. A tinkle. A clatter.

The grin on Slim's face wilted. "Oops. I believe I just shot out a winder glass."

Sure enough, several of the BBs had bounced off the floor and blown holes in two panes in the back window. Slim pushed himself out of the easy chair and walked over to examine the evidence. Naturally, I went with him.

As you may know, we dogs recognize that the Sharing of Pain is a very important part of our job. When our masters make bonehead mistakes, they need a loyal dog at their side to . . . well, to give them Looks of Greatest Sympathy, to wag our tails, and to assure them that, hey, anyone could have, uh, shot holes in a window. In his own house. With a slingshot. While hunting mice.

Sometimes it's hard to pull off Looks of Greatest Sympathy, because it's hard to keep from laughing. This was one of those deals. At such times, we have to impose Iron Discipline upon our laughing instincts.

Well, I wasn't laughing. Not me. I had been through all this before—maybe not a broken window, but things just as weird—and I didn't even crack a smile. I matched my expression to Slim's expression, and together our expressions expressed Deep Sorrow and Regret.

Yes, this was a sad evening for the ranch. Slim would have to stuff paper or chewing gum into the holes to keep out the rain.

But before he had the chance to do anything about it, the phone rang.

CHAPTER FIVE

A Mysterious Phone Call in the Night

So there we were, Slim and I, in the midst of a sorrowful inspection of the damaged windowpanes, when the phone rang.

Slim scowled. "Who could that be, calling in the middle of the dadgum night?"

He glanced down at me. What was I supposed to say? I didn't know who was calling. And it wasn't the middle of the night. It was maybe nine o'clock.

Slim headed for the phone in that slow walk of his. Oh, and he was muttering under his breath.

"Sometimes I think the world was better off when we didn't have any phones. A man could spend a quiet evening without all the . . . that's fine, ring all you want, I ain't going to walk one bit faster."

At last he found the phone and put the receiver to his ear. "Hello. Yes. Yes. Who is this? Oh, Joe. Didn't recognize your voice. Nothing much, just . . . doing a little house cleaning, me and the dogs." He gave me a wink. "What's up? Oh? That's not so good. Uh-huh. Yalp. Well, we'll keep an eye open for him. If he comes around, I'll try to pen him up. See you in the morning."

He hung up the receiver and stared at the floor. "I told him that big dog was going to be big trouble." His eyes came up. "That rottweiler jumped out of the pickup on the way home and Joe couldn't find him in the dark. Joe's coming back down tomorrow to look for him."

Was that a big deal? Not to me. I mean, I had gotten my point across to the mutt and I was pretty sure we would never see his face around our ranch again. Time and time again, history has proved that the best way to prevent trouble with strange dogs is to be firm with 'em the first time they show up. That's just what I had done, and I was so unconcerned and unworried about Bruiser that I sat down in the middle of the floor and began hacking at a flea just behind my left ear.

Hack, hack, hack.

Have we discussed the Hacking Procedure? We dogs use it on unruly fleas who are silly enough to bite us in sensitive spots, such as behind the ears. As you may know, fleas not only bite but they also steal blood. Some dogs put up with it because . . . I don't know why they put up with it. Because they're too lazy to take Flea Counter-measures, I suppose, but I don't put up with it, not for a minute.

Hack, hack, hack.

We have several Flea Countermeasures, and the one I use most often is the Hacking Procedure. In this procedure, the bitten dog drops his bottom side on the ground, or on the floor if he happens to be inside the house, which I was. Once he has achieved the Hacking Position, he selects one of his two hind legs for the job.

I know this may sound complicated, but bear with me.

He selects one of his two hind legs for the job. You're probably wondering why we use hind legs instead of front legs. Good question. The reason we use hind legs for this procedure is that front legs are just not capable of delivering a good, robust hack. Front paws are okay for your rubbing or scratching procedures, but fleas seldom respond to rubs or scratches.

They have to be *hacked*, and that's a job for a huge, muscular hind leg, of which I had two. See,

your hind legs are hinged in the middle, which means that with the proper training, an experienced dog can get just the right angle for his hack.

Hack, hack, hack.

I chose the left hind leg for the job. You're probably wondering, Why the left and not the right? Great question, and here's the scooby on that. In making our Hack Calculations, we follow a simple equation. (You might want to make a note of this.)

Left ear, left hind leg. Right ear, right hind leg.

That makes sense, doesn't it? If I had selected the right leg instead of the left, I would have found it difficult—maybe even impossible—to direct a lethal force of claws to the target area, because . . . I'm not sure why, actually, but it has something to do with some very complicated laws of physics and we don't have time for that.

Just take my word for it: you can't hack a left ear with a right leg.

Okay, now let's put this all together and see how it works.

Hack, hack, hack. Hack, hack, hack.

Did you notice that I increased the velocity of my hack? I did, and you're probably wondering . . .

Huh?

Slim was standing over me, glaring down with stern eyes. All at once I became aware of several . . . quite a few . . . were those dog hairs floating in the atmosphere of the, uh, living room?

"Hank, I told you not to shed hair all over my pretty house."

Well, yes, sure, but there was a reason for the, uh, hairs. See, when you hack a flea, you just naturally hack up a few . . . well, hairs, dog hairs. And what's a hair to do once it has been hacked up and released into the atomsphere? It floats around. It's a natural, organic process, part of nature's plan for the . . .

He nudged me with his toe and shot a bony finger toward the door. "That's it, bozo, outside. You can shed hair on the porch."

What? Wait, I could explain . . . what did he expect me to do, sit there and let the stupid flea bite my ear off and drain my entire body of bodily fluids? Hey, that was my blood, and I wasn't going to let some sniveling little flea . . .

He nudged me again with his foot, this time quite a bit harder. "Out."

Fine. I could take a hint. If he didn't care any more about his dogs than that, if he expected us to sit around like ninnies and be devoured by biting hypodermiac fleas . . . fine.

I would just march myself outside and spend the night on his broken-down, two-bit porch. And

I would never come back into his slummy old house again. Never. Come winter, when the north wind howled and groaned, he would want a friend to share his fire, but it wouldn't be me, Charlie.

I would be out on the porch, suffering in silence and hacking all the fleas I wanted to hack.

And the next time he wanted a loyal dog to join him on a mouse hunt, I would be busy. When he called my name and begged me to share his boring life, I would give him a heartless stare and say, "No thanks. I'm hacking fleas and I'm sure you wouldn't approve."

Holding my head at a proud angle, I marched myself to the front door, then beamed him a killer look that said, "Is it possible that you're really doing this?"

Our eyes met. "Well, pooch, I'm sure going to miss you tonight—all the dog hairs and bad smells. Y'all have a sweet dream, hear? And don't even think about barking all night, 'cause come morning, I won't be my usual charming self."

Usual charming self? Ha. That was a laugh. But he didn't need to worry about me barking in the night. Dogs who bark at night are on the job, and I had no intention of working the night shift after being thrown out of house and home over something as silly as a few dog hairs.

No sir, I intended to sleep, and if the monsters came up around the house in the dead of night, Slim could bark at them himself.

With that, I turned my nose toward the door. Slim pushed it open and I marched outside. He would be sorry, of course, but he had done this to himself. I couldn't be blamed.

Once out on the porch, I turned around, sat down, and stared at him through the screen. I beamed him Looks of Deepest Tragedy and Betrayal. He noticed.

"Are you going to sit there all night, staring at me through the screen door?"

I might, yes, I sure might.

"Well, enjoy yourself, 'cause I'm going to bed. Oh, and don't worry. Stub Tail will be joining you just as soon as I flush him out from under my bed. Nighty-night."

He left. Two minutes later, he returned with Stub Tail and tossed him out with me in the creel cool world. Cold cruel world, I should say, although it wasn't actually cold, this being . . . never mind.

Drover landed on the porch beside me. He avoided my gaze and curled up into a little ball.

"Well, I see you got thrown out. What did you do this time?"

"Nothing. I didn't do anything. I was just hid-

ing under the bed and minding my own business, and the next thing I knew, Slim threw me out."

"Was it possible that you were shedding hairs under his bed?"

"Well . . . I don't think so. I wasn't trying to shed any hairs."

"Hmm, yes. This is sounding very familiar, Drover, for you see, I was thrown out on the same phony charge."

"You were?"

"Yes. I was minding my own business and hacking at a flea, when Slim blundered in and accused me of shedding hairs. Maybe I hacked off a hair or two, but that's no reason for throwing us out."

"It's not fair. I thought he was our friend."

"Yes, and some friend he turned out to be. Our friendship collapsed under the weight of two or three measly dog hairs. Maybe we should run away, Drover, just pack our bugs and disappear into the night. That might teach him a lesson on how to treat his loyal dogs, the cad."

"Yeah, but then we'd have to leave."

"Well . . . yes, of course we'd have to leave. That's the whole point."

"Yeah, but it's awful dark, and you know how I am about the dark."

I beamed him a scorching glare. "This is a matter of principle, Drover. Are you going to let your irrational fear of the dark stand in the way of our search for justice?"

"How far would we have to go?"

"We'd have to go . . . I'm not sure. I guess that would depend on how badly our feelings are hurt over this deal. I'm feeling pretty outraged. Maybe we ought to go . . . oh, say twenty or twenty-five miles."

I heard him gulp. "In the dark?"

"Of course in the dark, unless you want to carry a flashlight in your mouth."

"I don't have a flashlight."

"Neither do I, so that settles it." There was a

long moment of silence. "Okay, what about something shorter, say five miles?"

"That's still a long way."

"Drover, if we're going to quit our jobs and run away from home, we need to *go somewhere*. Otherwise, Slim will never learn from his mistake. He needs to feel some pain for this. If we can't go at least five miles, we should just forget it."

"Yeah, but . . . what about coyotes?"

I gave that some thought. "Coyotes could be a . . . uh . . . problem."

"They're pretty scary guys."

"Good point. Okay, suppose we go only one mile? Maybe that would . . ." Just then, we heard the howl of a distant coyote. "Or better yet, maybe we could just hike down to the barn and spend the night there."

"You think that would be far enough?"

"Oh, sure. It would deprive Slim of our warmth and presence on his porch. When he wakes up in the morning, he'll look out here and see that we're gone. It just might give him such a scare that he'll change his ways before it's too late. What do you say to that?"

"Well, I guess I can do it. Are you sure it's safe?"

"Of course I'm sure. What could happen to us between here and the barn?"

"Well . . . okay, I guess I can make it, if this old leg'll stay with me."

"Forget the leg, son. Saddle up and let's move out." I jacked myself up off the porch and beamed a cold glare at the house. "Good-bye, old house. Good-bye, Slim. We're quitting our jobs and leaving this hateful place, never to return until tomorrow. If the monsters come out . . . too bad. We're signing off. You're on your own."

And with that, we left the porch and began our long and dangerous journey to Slim's raggedy little barn.

A Phantom
in the Darkness

You might think this wasn't such a big deal, me and Drover running away from home and going . . . well, two hundred feet to the northwest. That's how far the barn was from Slim's shack, see, but let me hasten to point out that it was dark, very dark, and more than a little bit spooky.

So going to the barn was a bigger deal than you might have supposed. As we picked our way through the inky darkness, Drover began to moan and groan.

"Hank, I wish you hadn't said what you said about monsters. Do you really think there might be some out here?"

"It's always a possibility, son. They've been reported in this area, I can tell you that much."

"What kind?"

"Oh, let me think. A tree monster, a bush monster, and a couple of lightning monsters. We know they inhabit this part of the ranch."

"Gosh. Do you reckon we might see one?"

"Not likely. I checked Smelloradar and Earatory Scanners, and they're both clear. I'd say the monsters are working another part of the ranch tonight."

"Oh good. Boy, I'd sure hate to . . . did you hear that?"

"Hear what?" I stopped and listened. "I don't hear anything."

"Well, I heard something. Listen. Hear that clicking sound?"

I lifted my Earatory Scanners and swept a circle for sounds. And sure enough, I began picking up a mysterious clicking sound.

"There it is, Drover. I don't want to alarm you, but my instruments are picking up . . . yes, there it is, a clear signal."

"Oh my gosh, I knew we should have stayed on the porch!"

"Hush. I'm trying to run diagnostics on this." I studied the huge lighted screen of my mind. "This isn't looking good, son."

"What is it?"

"We're picking up a clear signal of . . . *teeth clicking.*"

"Teeth clicking! Oh my gosh, it's a monster, help, murder, Mayday!"

"Shhh. Control yourself. Be professional." I must admit that I was having a little trouble with this myself. I mean, when you're out there in the dark and you hear . . . GULP.

Drover was moaning again. "Do monsters have teeth?"

"Affirmative."

"Do they ever . . . click their teeth?"

"Sometimes they do, yes, but not very often— only when they're about to . . ."

"Attack and tear something to shreds?"

"I didn't want to put it that way, Drover, but yes. According to our reports, they click their teeth when they . . . uh . . . do the things you mentioned. And I'm afraid we . . . wait a minute, hold everything."

"I'm trying to hold it, but if this gets any scarier, I'm going to lose it."

"Shhhh. Listen." I studied the sound again. "It seems to be close, don't you think?"

"Y-y-y-yes, I'm af-f-f-fraid s-s-so."

"It seems to be . . ." My body wilted and the air hissed out of my lungs. "Drover, the sound is coming from *you*. Have you been clicking your teeth?"

"Me? No, I don't think so. My teeth have been chattering, but they haven't clicked."

"Clicking, chattering, it's all the same. You're the cause of this, and I must warn you not to click or chatter your teeth anymore."

"Yeah, but I'm scared, and when I'm scared, my teeth chatter."

"Well, stop it. You're sending confusing signals that mess up our instruments."

"I want to go back to the porch!"

"Oh, rubbish. There's no monster out here. Dry up and let's get on with this."

We resumed our creeping journey through the darkness. We had gone another twenty steps when Drover whispered, "Hank, I hear footsteps behind me."

I stopped and heaved a sigh. "Drover, please. We have a very important mission here."

"Yeah, but I heard footsteps. Listen."

I listened. "I hear nothing, absolutely nothing."

"Me too, but I'm almost sure I heard footsteps when we were walking."

I couldn't help chuckling. "When we were walking? That's a crucial piece of evidence, Drover. Shall I explain? Okay, when we walk, our feet make . . . you supply the answer."

"Uh . . . footsteps?"

"Exactly. Very good."

"Yeah, but these were behind me."

"I'm getting there, Drover, just relax. Consider the way your body is put together. On one end, we have your head, right?"

"I think so."

"And upon your head sits a pair of . . . what?"

"Let's see. Ears?"

"Ears, yes, which are the devices that pick up sounds. Now, let's move to the other end of your body. What do we find there?"

"Well . . . a stub tail and my bohunkus."

"Right, and below those parts, we have . . . what?"

"I don't know, I'm all confused."

"We have your hind legs, Drover, and attached to the end of your hind legs are your hind feet, and when you walk, your hind feet make footsteps. Are you getting it yet?"

"Yeah, but the footsteps were behind me."

I rolled my eyes. "Of course they were, numbskull. You were hearing your own footsteps! Now cut out the nonsense and let's get on with this."

"Yeah, but . . ."

"Shhhh! No more. Silence."

We resumed our trek down to the . . . footsteps?

Heavy footsteps? I stopped. Drover stopped. The heavy footsteps continued, then stopped.

My mouth was suddenly dry. "Drover, I don't want to alarm you, but I'm now picking up those footsteps you mentioned."

"I thought they were mine."

"These *weren't* yours, and unless I'm badly mistaken..." I cut my eyes from side to side. "Drover, one last question. When we were inside the house, Slim got a phone call. It was something about...a dog. Bruiser. Did you happen to hear what Slim said?"

"Well, let's see here. I think he said ..." The silence that followed was deadly. "Hank, you don't reckon ..."

It was then that we heard the burst of wicked laughter behind us. The hair on my back and neck stood straight up.

"Drover, was that you laughing?"

"N-n-no."

"And it wasn't me. Do you see what this means?"

Then came the eerie voice from the darkness. "Hi, fellas. Out for a little stroll? I guess you thought I was gone, huh? Well, darn the luck. I came back."

"Drover, we have a problem. And I hear water running."

"It's me. I want to go home!"

"Back to the porch, son. Go to Turbo Five and don't speak to any strangers. Let's hit it!"

I went to Full Flames and Turbo Five on all engines and . . . BONK! . . . ran into something big and hairy. I bounced off it and went streaking through the darkness and didn't slow down until I had made it to the safety of the front porch.

There, I went straight into a Code Three Barking Sequence. Have we discussed the CTBS? Maybe not. Big barks, massive barks. Barks that echo through the night, barks that are calculated to alert the house and call our human friends to the rescue.

This was no time for timid barks, fellers. We had to sound the alarm and let Slim know that Bruiser was back and on the prowl, and if Slim didn't get himself out of bed and hurry up . . .

The front door opened, thank goodness, and there stood Slim in his . . . yipes . . . in his shorts, with hair falling into his puffy eyes and a ferocious expression on his face. He pushed open the screen door and leveled a finger at the end of my nose.

"Hank, if you'll shut up your dadgum barking, I'll try not to do what I'm thinking of doing. You hear?"

Yes sir, but . . .

"Now go to sleep. First you trash my house with your hair, then you wake me up with all that frazzling noise."

He slammed the door. Silence moved over us like a dark cloud of smoke. I could hear Drover's clacking teeth beside me. And then . . . *Bruiser's heavy footsteps were moving up the walk and toward the porch!*

There was just a glimmer of moonlight, enough so that I could make out the profile of . . . good grief, that was a huge rottweiler, as big as a bear! Did

I dare activate the Code Three Barking Sequence again?

My mind was racing. We were trapped between Slim's irritation and Bruiser's massive presence. I had to choose my poison. I chose to face Slim's irritation. I had faced it before, and I knew that no matter how mad he got at us dogs, he would never eat us.

With Bruiser, I wasn't so sure.

I launched myself into another barrage of massive barking. "Slim, help, get out of bed, he's back, Bruiser's back, the raging rottweiler's out here in your front yard, so could you please . . ."

It worked. At last my barking got his attention and convinced him that we were in a desperate situation. It had taken him long enough, but . . . oh well. Better late than tardy.

The door opened. My confidence came rushing back when I heard his foot land on the porch. A sneer worked its way across my mouth, and I turned myself to face the darkened yard, in which I knew Bruiser was lurking, even though I couldn't actually see him.

And you might find this hard to believe, but I was feeling so good about this that I decided it was time to send a warning to Mister Rottweiler.

"Okay, potlicker, I can now reveal that you've

walked right into our trap. Surprised? Ha. What a dumbbell you turned out to be. Did you think you could just walk onto my ranch without permission and get away with it? It's called trespassing, and you're now in big . . ."

SPLOSH!

You won't believe what happened.

CHAPTER SEVEN

Bruiser Returns

There I was on the front porch, barking my very heart out and trying to get the message through Slim's thick skull that a raging rottweiler was standing in his yard—all of that, and guess what he did.

He drenched me with a pot of cold water.

See? I told you that you wouldn't believe it, and sure enough, you didn't. I couldn't believe it either.

I mean, there I was in the trenches, in the Foxholes of Life, in a very dangerous combat situation, doing my job and trying to protect his house from a raging rottweiler—and he stepped out on the porch and threw a pot of water on me! Slim did.

Oh, and then he said—this is an exact quote—

he said, "Hank, I've run out of nice ways to tell you to quit barking. Now shut up and let me get some sleep."

BAM! The door closed and he was gone.

As water dribbled off the end of my nose, I sensed that my relationship with Slim had taken a plunge into a new direction. Up to then, it had been a mixture of good and bad. From now on, it would be a mixture of bad and worse.

I would have to resign, of course, and leave the ranch forever. Slim and I would never see each other again. I had no other choice. You can't humiliate the Head of Ranch Security and expect him to go on as though nothing had happened.

No, it was over. My friendship with Slim Chance came to a bitter end the very moment he dumped that pot of . . .

HUH?

Laughter? I heard a deep, wicked laugh coming from the direction of the yard, and suddenly I was reminded that . . . uh . . . I had recently mouthed off to a very large . . . gulk . . . and yes, it appeared that we had more pressing problems than my souring relations with Slim.

Bruiser was out there in the darkness. I still couldn't see him, but now I could hear him breathing. Your rottweilers are sloppy breathers, did you know that? They are. They snort and slop when they breathe, and on a dark night, it sounds pretty eerie.

I ran my gaze through the darkness. "Drover, can you hear me?"

No answer, then . . . "I hear you."

"Good. Listen carefully. Our situation is looking grim. Number one, I have reason to believe that there's a dangerous rottweiler in front of the house."

"I thought you said he was a scaredy cat."

"We may have gotten some bad information on that, son. Okay, number two, we barked the house for reinforcements, remember? They're not coming. We're cut off from the main column and we're on our own."

"Yeah, I know."

"Okay, number three, we need a volunteer to lead a scouting mission into the yard. We must find out what we're facing here. And number four, we've talked about how I need to be giving you more responsibility. Remember?"

"Oh yeah."

"Well, this would be a great opportunity for you to, uh, prove what you're made of."

"Yeah, but I already know. Spaghetti."

"Spaghetti? Drover, are you saying . . . Drover,

where are you? Give me your exact location."

"I'm on top of the woodpile."

"On top . . . Drover, get down here at once. Our porch is under assault."

"Yeah, and it could be under a pepper and I'd still be up here."

"What? Are you refusing to obey a direct order? Drover, I command you to answer my question!"

"Can't hear you, Hank, you'll have to yell. I must have some wax in my ear."

"You've got wax in your brain, and as your commanding officer, I demand . . ."

Bruiser's ugly laugh cut through the darkness. "It's looking pretty bad, ain't it, boys? Two mutts on the porch and neither one has the guts to stand up and fight."

Did I dare respond? Yes, I had to. I would deal with Drover later.

"Oh, Bruiser, is that you? Hey, how's it going? Pretty dark tonight, huh?"

"Yeah, real dark. Too dark for a town dog like me to be out walking around. You know, I might get lost or something. What I really need is a nice porch to sleep on, know what I mean?"

"A porch? Yes, porches are, uh, nice, they sure are, and, hey, I just remembered, the next house down the creek has a great porch. Bigger than this one. Better, much better. Glider swing, pillows, you name it. Great porch. Maybe you could . . ."

"Naaa. I don't need the exercise . . . even though some smart guy once said I walk like a fat duck."

"Fat duck? Now who would . . . oh, you mean me? Ha, ha. That was a joke, Bruiser, honest, just a joke. Good wholesome humor, but no kidding, I think you'd love that porch down the creek. It's worth the walk."

"Naaa. I'm scared of the dark. And besides, I like your porch."

"You do? Well, uh, thanks. That's a nice compliment, although the porch actually belongs to Slim, and I'm not sure he'd want you, uh, sleeping here. On his porch. Don't you see."

"Yeah? Well, bark him out of bed again and we'll ask."

"No, I think not. We tried that and . . . well, he asked that we not disturb him."

Bruiser was moving up the steps. I could hear his sloppy breathing. "Well, gee, what can we do? I mean, I sure wouldn't want to sleep here if I'm not welcome."

"It's nothing personal. He just doesn't allow . . . uh . . . strange dogs, see. Sleeping on the porch. I'm sure you understand."

"Yeah? Well, here's the way I figure it. I'm going

to sleep on your porch. The only question is, how many dogs do I have to kill before I do it?"

I tried to swallow the cotton and wool inside my mouth. "How many dogs ... Bruiser, may I ask you a personal question? We were told ... that is, we received a tip that, well, maybe you're not as mean as you, uh, seem to be. Is there any ... well, truth to that?"

I heard him laugh. "Well, now, I guess you could bet your life on it and find out."

"Oh no, that's not necessary, really. No, it's a big porch, Bruiser, and I'm sure there's plenty of ..."

"I have an idea. I'll sleep on the porch and you sleep on top of the woodpile with your buddy. How does that sound?"

He was right beside me now. I could feel his hot dragon breath on my face. "Actually, Bruiser, I think it would look bad. Undignified. See, I'm Head of Ranch ..."

He cut loose with a low, deep growl.

"On second thought, that would be fine. The woodpile would be great. No problem. Drover, make way, I'm coming up."

I leaped up on top of the woodpile. Drover was there, of course, and he greeted me with, "Oh hi. What are you doing up here?"

"Never mind. Scoot over. It seems we're going to be sharing this bunk."

"Oh good, but I thought . . ."

"Never mind. Scoot over and dry up."

He skeet over and dried up, and silence fell over our little compound. The silence didn't last long. Drover, the little goof, fell right off to sleep (how could he sleep at such a time?) and began making his usual orchestra of weird sounds—wheezing, whistling, honking, and grunting in his sleep. As if that weren't bad enough, Bruiser had his own set of noises. Remember what I said about rottweilers being sloppy breathers? Well, guess what they do in their sleep. They snore. He snored like a ten-ton truck! No kidding, it was terrible.

Who could sleep in the midst of such noise? I'll tell you who: Drover and Bruiser. Oh, and Slim— Mister Couldn't Sleep for All the Noise and Doused Me with a Pot of Water. Now that we had a rottweiler King Kong occupying our porch, Slim slept like a rock.

A great help he turned out to be.

Well, I knew I would be up for the rest of the night. I mean, not only was the noise unbearable, but I had many things on my mind—such as what Slim would say in the morning if he found the entire Security Division . . . uh . . . asleep on the heights of the woodpile. It wouldn't look good, not good at all, and worrying about such detonks is just the sort of thunk that keeps me awonk all nop.

All *night*, I should say.

See, I spend a lop of my toink worrying abonk such tiny derails . . . details. My mind is very okra, don't you sleep, and it konks me awonking snork murk . . . boiled turnips . . . chasing rabbits . . . through the pillow feathers . . . zzzzzzzzzzzzzzz.

Okay, maybe I finally dozed off, and the next thing I knew . . . HUH? I heard a door open and found myself staring at . . . a scarecrow. That was odd. Scarecrows lived in gardens, right? And this was no garden. This was . . .

I blinked my eyes and studied my surrenders . . . my surroundings, shall we say. The porch. I was lying on the porch . . . on the woodpile, actually, and the scarecrow turned out to be Slim. The events of the previous evening came rushing back to my memory banks, and I found myself beaming . . . uh . . . Looks of Great Embarrassment toward Slim. And giving my tail Slow Taps, as if to say, "I know this looks odd, but hear me out, I can explain everything."

He blinked his soggy red eyes. "What are you fools doing on the woodpile?" Then his gaze slid away from me and fell upon the sleeping monster on our porch. His eyebrows shot up. "Good honk, it's Bruiser. Is that what you dogs were barking about?"

Oh brother.

Just then, Bruiser woke up and raised his head. He looked straight into Slim's eyes. Rottweilers do that, you know. They have a way of staring directly at someone and showing not one hint of fear. They just *stare*, and you don't have any idea what's going through their minds.

That must have unnerved old Slim, because he backed into the house, and when he returned a moment later, he was armed with a catch rope. I felt an impulse to stand up and cheer, but I didn't, because I knew that we were about to enter into a very dangerous moment. Let's see if I can describe it.

From where I was sitting, it appeared that Slim had chosen the rope as his weapon of choice. See, a cowboy's rope can be either a catching device or a pretty good substitute for a club, depending on the situation. I'd seen Slim kill big rattlesnakes with his rope—pull the loop down to a knot, swing the knot around on six feet of rope, and then WHACK! You could crush a rattlesnake's head with one shot.

Without taking his eyes off of Bruiser, he built

a small loop and took a step in Bruiser's direction. Bruiser's eyes never moved or wavered. Slim started talking in a voice that was soft but firm.

"Now Bruiser, you've lost your way in the world, and I mean you no harm. I'm going to ease this loop around your neck so's you'll be around when Joe McCall gets here to pick you up. It's for your own good and nobody's going to hurt you—unless you decide to play King Kong again, and then, son, the fur will fly. Yours."

Slim took another step. Bruiser didn't flinch or move or show any emotion at all. Their eyes were locked together. Drover woke up, saw the scene unfolding, and covered his eyes with his paws.

Slim took another step. Bruiser stared. The tension grew and grew. I could hardly stand to watch it. I had a feeling that something terrible was about to happen and . . .

This is getting too scary. I don't think we'd better go on.

CHAPTER EIGHT

Much Too Scary
for Most Readers

What? You're still here? I guess you think I'm
going to change my mind and tell you the
rest of the story, huh?

Nope, can't do it. Sorry. It's just too tense and
scary. Think of the kids. It might scare 'em so
badly, they'd . . . I don't know what might happen.
We'll skip over the bad part and go on to something else.

It's for your own good, honest.

Okay, here we go. It was morning on the ranch
and there was no raging rottweiler on the porch,
not even a sign of one. Not only was Bruiser not
there, but we'd never heard of him and maybe he
didn't even exist. Yes, that was it. There was no
such dog as Bruiser, and even if there had been . . .

Oh, what the heck, maybe you can handle it. Shall we give it a try? Okay, but don't blame me if you get scared all the way into next week. Here we go. Hang on.

There they were, Slim and Bruiser, heading for a faceful confrontation. Fateful, I should say, and neither showed any sign of backing down. Gulp. But one of them had to back down. In this game of nerves, there could be only one winner.

Slim held the loop out in front of him. Bruiser didn't look at the loop. His steely eyes were fixed on Slim. Closer and closer . . .

At that very moment, when it appeared that Slim and Bruiser were heading down a path of no return, we heard the rattle of a pickup coming our way. It was Joe McCall. Bruiser turned his head and looked toward the sound. Slim eased the loop over his head and snugged it up—not tight, but snug.

I held my breath and waited to see what Bruiser would do. He . . .

You won't believe this. He felt the rope, looked up at Slim, and . . . *began wagging his stub tail!* Slim leaned down and rubbed him behind the ears.

"That's better. Nice dog." He straightened up and made a low whistling sound. "Whew! I guess he ain't as mean as he looks." He turned to me and grinned. "It's safe for you heroes to come down off the woodpile now."

Was he suggesting . . . hey, for his information, I had chosen to sleep on top of the woodpile because it was cooler up there. It had nothing, almost nothing at all, to do with any uneasy feelings I might have had about . . .

Hey, Bruiser was nothing but a big windbag, and I'd known it the minute I'd first laid eyes on him. Scared of cats. Scared of his face in the mirror. All bark and no bite, all talk and no fight. Why, he was just lucky I was such a kind and generous dog, otherwise, I might have . . .

I hopped down off the woodpile and walked boldly up to Mister Phony Rottweiler and put my nose in his left flank. He growled. Big deal. I gave him one right back, and mine was twice as awesome as his.

"You'd best keep your distance, cowdog."

"Oh yeah? Tell that to Drover. He might be impressed."

Before I could give the big chicken liver the thrashing he so richly deserved, Joe McCall rushed in and snapped a chain around his neck and led him away to the pickup. When I saw that the chain was secured to the racks of the pickup, I dived off the porch and went streaking out into the yard.

Slim tried to hold me back, but my thirst for revenge was just too great. I gave the mutt a burst of Savage Warning Barks.

"And let that be a lesson to you, Mister Phony Rottweiler. If you ever set foot on this ranch again, you won't be walking like a fat duck anymore. You won't even be walking, because you won't have any legs!"

Pretty impressive, huh? You bet. I got him told, yes sir, and the big lug was so shocked, so scared, so amazed, he didn't even bark back. He just gave me that ugly stare and rumbled, "You're such a loser."

They drove away. I lobbed a few more barks at 'em from the gravel drive, just to make sure they didn't stop or loiter on their way out. Then I turned and marched proudly back to the porch. Slim was there, leaning against a porch post and running a toothpick through his teeth. I could see that he was impressed.

"You know, Hank, there's certain times when a dog ought to keep his mouth shut. But some dogs learn harder than others."

Okay, so maybe he wasn't impressed. Did I care? Heck no. I had done my job and had sent the rottweiler packing, and it was just too bad that Slim didn't appreciate the high quality of my work. He was the same guy, you might remember, who had dumped a pot of water on me in the middle of the night. That's how much he knew about Ranch Security.

Zero.

Well, by then it was past eight o'clock and time to start the day's work. Slim hooked up the stock trailer, saddled a horse, and loaded him in the trailer. As he was walking toward the pickup, he saw me and Drover sitting in front of the barn.

"I'm going up on the flats to check on them steers. Y'all want to tag along?"

Me? Tag along with *him*, after he'd dumped that pot of water on me? Ha! No thanks. I had better things to do and better friends to do 'em with.

He shrugged and climbed into the pickup. "Dumb dogs."

Drover shot me a glance. "Know what? I think I'll go. How about you?"

"Not me, pal. Slim and I aren't on the best of terms right now. I think it would do him some good to spend the day alone."

"Yeah, but it's kind of boring around here."

"Not for me, son. Excitement is where you find it, and I seem to find quite a lot of it, no matter where I am."

Slim started the motor. Drover began edging toward the pickup. "Well, I think I'll go. See you around." He hopped up into the back.

"That's fine, Drover. You go and I'll stay here and enjoy my own company."

"Bye, Hank."

They pulled away. What a relief. At last I was rid of the little squeak box and could look forward to spending my whole day . . . come to think of it, there wasn't all that much to do around Slim's place. I mean, no chickens to chase, no cats to humble, no . . .

I trotted out and followed the pickup. "Drover, on second thought, I might go along for the ride. Hold up a second."

"Well, I'm not driving. You'll have to get Slim's attention."

"You can forget that. Slim and I aren't on speaking terms right now."

"Well, I don't know what to do. Bye now. Have a good day."

Okay, so I had to swallow my pride and trot along beside the pickup to . . . well, inform Slim that I had reconsidered his offer and had decided . . .

He saw me trotting beside the pickup, I knew he saw me, but did he pull over and let me in? Oh no. That would have been too simple and easy. He made me trot and run a quarter mile before he finally stopped in the middle of the road. And then, of course, he had to make a big deal out of it.

"Make up your mind, pooch, I ain't running a taxi service. If you're going with me, get in."

See? That's all the thanks I got for . . . oh well. One of us had to show some maturity, and as usual, it had to be me. I hopped into the back and growled Drover out of my place of honor in the middle of the spare tire.

We turned right on the county road and picked up speed. The wind began blowing my ears and tongue around. It blew my tongue around because my mouth was open, because that's how we dogs air-condition our bodies in hot weather. We pant, see, and somehow that panting action cools us down.

So I closed my eyes and let the wind tease and tickle my ears, while it also served the purpose of cooling down my . . . dog hairs? I opened my eyes and noticed a bunch of dog hairs swirling around in the air. Several of them . . . a bunch of them had landed on my tongualary region, forcing me to close my mouth and spit them out.

I beamed a glare at my assistant. Over the roar of the wind, I yelled, "Hey, quit shedding hair! They're getting in my mouth."

He grinned. "Yeah, I was under Slim's bed, but it sounded like fun."

"Mouth. My mouth."

"You killed a mouse?"

"You're getting hair in my mouth."

"You got a mouse in your mouth?"

"No, I'm getting your hair in my mouth. Hair! Your hair is swirling around."

"Squirrels around? I thought they were mice."

"What?"

"The squirrels. Were they inside the house?"

"Those were mice. MICE."

"Yeah, squirrels are nice. I've always liked 'em."

This wasn't working. I heaved a sigh and pushed

myself out of my spare-tire throne and lumbered over to the runt. I put my mouth at the entrance of his ear canal and raised my voice.

"I said, YOU ARE SHEDDING HAIR. THE HAIR IS GETTING IN MY MOUTH."

He crumpled up like a burned spider and put his paws over his ears. "Don't yell! It hurts my ears, and I hate to be yelled at in the morning."

"Okay, then try reading my lips. Look at my mouth."

He looked at my mouth. "I'll be derned. Did you know you've got dog hairs in your mouth?"

"What? You'll have to speak up. I can't hear anything in this wind."

He put his mouth next to my ear. "DID YOU KNOW YOU'VE GOT DOG HAIRS IN YOUR MOUTH?"

His screeching was so loud, it caused my earatory circuits to short out. "Don't yell in my ear, you bonehead! I'm not deaf! Now, what did you say? I'll try to read your . . . Drover, you've got dog hairs all over your lips. Were you aware of that?"

"I know. I think they're yours. Maybe you're shedding hair in this heat."

For a moment I stared into the emptiness of his eyes. I felt exhausted, worn down by the forces of chaos. "Drover, sometimes I get the feeling that it's impossible to communicate with you. Please don't ever speak to me again."

"Oh, that's okay. A few little hairs won't hurt."

"Drover, sometimes I think I hate you."

"No, I ate first thing this morning. I couldn't hold another bite, but thanks."

I turned away from the little lunatic and staggered back to my spare tire.

I curled up and closed my eyes for the remainder of the ride.

Make no mistake about it. Drover is a WEIRD little mutt.

Slim and I
Check Cattle

I opened my eyes and saw that we had reached the Barnett place, a pasture up on the flats that Loper had leased for the summer.

The pickup lurched to a stop. I rose from the spare tire and went straight into a Yawning and Stretching procedure. There, that felt better. The toxic vapors Drover had unleashed inside my brain had drifted away, leaving me whole and sound again.

I was ready to go to work.

Slim unloaded Snips, his horse for the day, and tightened the cinch. He swung up into the saddle and we set out on our mission, counting and checking two hundred yearling steers that were summering on grass. Hey, this was my kind of work.

We headed east in a long trot, Slim and I did, and I noticed that Drover stayed at the pickup. Why? Because he's a little weenie. Because he doesn't know beans about the cattle business and doesn't care to learn. Because the day was hot and he wanted to lie around in the shade.

Oh, and because his leg was giving him fits, or so he claimed. But that was okay with me. I'd had all of Drover I could stand for one day.

You know why Drover is always bored? Because he's locked inside a body with *himself*.

Slim trotted his horse for a few hundred yards, until we came to a little bunch of steers, and then he slowed Snips to a walk.

He got a good count and wrote the number down in the palm of his left hand. We moved on to the next bunch, and he went through the same procedure. By that time, he had tallied 187 steers, and all we had to do was find the remaining ten. Twelve. Thirteen.

We mushed on to the east. There, under a little rise, we found a bunch lying in some tall grass and sunflowers.

I knew my part in this deal and did it. I trotted into the middle of the steers and started growling orders. "Okay, you lazy bums, stand up and face inspection. Anybody sick? Bloated? Got pinkeye?

Move around, let's get a good look at you."

Pretty impressive, huh? You bet it was. I doubt that Slim could have done the job without me there to help him.

I growled 'em up and stirred 'em around, and Slim got his count. The only problem was that he came up one short. We rode through the whole pasture again and he made another count, and he was still one short. He leaned back in the saddle, tipped his hat to the back of his head, and chewed on his lip.

"I guess we'd better ride out this draw. Hank, walk through them tall weeds and check 'em out. If you find that missing steer, there's liable to be a bonus for you."

Bonus? All right, heck of a deal. Let's see, what would it be? A big, fresh sirloin steak? Yes, that would be nice. Slim knew my position on sirloin steaks: I love 'em. Or maybe . . .

"Hank, quit daydreaming and get to work. In this heat, I'm a-losing my ambition."

Okay, fine, only I wasn't "daydreaming." I was merely . . . planning out my strategy for finding the steer. Hey, we dogs don't just blunder into our work. We need a little time to plan and think through our, uh, business.

Sirloin steak would be fine.

I put my nose to the ground and plunged into the heavy growth of sunflowers, weeds, and other varieties of vegetation that grew in the bottom of the draw. In this kind of situation, we usually switch our targeting mechanisms over to Smelloradar, for the simple reason that . . . ACHOO! . . . those weeds were covered with dust and pollen and . . . ACHOO! . . . and that stuff can sure mess up our . . . ACHOO! . . . Smelloradar.

See, toward the middle of summer, certain varieties of weeds . . . ACHOO! . . . give off large amounts of pollen. You have your ragweeds, your pigweeds, your . . . ACHOO! . . . sunflowers, your bindweed, and all those other . . . ACHOO! . . . stupid, stinking weeds whose names I don't . . . ACHOO! . . . know, and don't care to know.

ACHOO!

And as I say, when a dog dives into the middle of 'em and goes into Deep Sniff on the . . . ACHOO! . . . Smelloradar, they can sure mess up his . . .

Through watering eyes, I noticed that Slim was grinning down at me. "Heh. Are them weeds a little dusty?"

Of course they were dusty. I wasn't sneezing just for the fun of it. They were also loaded with pollen.

"Well, hurry up. The ranch ain't paying you to sneeze, and I'm getting hot."

Oh brother. You see how much sympathy we get? None. Zero. You volunteer for a hazardous job and then . . . never mind.

I plunged back into the jungle of poisonous weeds and resumed my Search Procedure, only this time I cancelled the Deep Sniff. See, by this time I had figured out that if a guy breathes through his mouth instead of his nose, he won't be attacked by the . . . COUGH, COUGH . . . sneezing viruses or by the clouds of obnoxious . . . HARK, HACK . . . dust particles.

Sneezing, don't you know, is triggered by the noselary region, so if a guy starts breathing through his mouth . . . HARK, HACK, HONK . . . he can die of lung rot instead of nose rot, and I'd had just about all the stinking weeds I could stand for one day.

If Slim wanted someone to check out those weeds, by George he could climb off his horse and do it himself.

I pointed myself toward daylight and staggered through the . . .

There he was. The steer, the missing steer. He was lying in the weeds, directly in front of me, and you won't believe this part. You thought he was sick? Had pneumonia? Pinkeye? Scours? No sir, what he had was *a bucket over his head!* Because of the bucket he was not only blind, but he couldn't see, and he had wandered away from the other cattle.

And I had found him. Pretty impressive, huh? You bet it was. Slim pulled the bucket off, released the little dummy, and we were done.

We were a pretty good team, Slim and I, and I had decided to forget about the Water Incident of

the previous night. I could hardly wait for my bonus. Did he have a steak tucked away in his pocket? Maybe not, but . . . okay, a nice strip of beef jerky. Jerky is made of steak, right? Jerky would be fine.

He saw me waiting for my reward. He reached into his jeans pocket . . . yes, yes, this was going well, it would be a nice hunk of . . . my whole body quivered with antsipitation . . . anticipation, shall we say, and my tail began to whack itself on the . . .

He gave his head a shake. "I'm out of beef jerky, pooch. How about a nice fat grasshopper?"

I stared at him in disbelief. *A nice fat grasshopper!* What kind of crooked deal was this? Dogs didn't eat . . .

He climbed into the saddle and headed back to the pickup. That was it. No steak, no jerky, not even a "thank you, buddy." Sometimes I think this job is . . . oh well.

Upon reaching the pickup, we made a shocking discovery. The pickup had a flat tire. Slim moaned and groaned about having to change a flat tire in the heat, but there was nobody else to do it, so he grabbed the highlift jack and the spinner tire tool and went to work. I sat in the shade and enjoyed every moment of his suffering. It served him right for cheating me out of my reward.

At last he got the spare tire put on and loaded the jack and the flat tire on the pickup bed. He wiped the sweat out of his eyes and took a gulp of air.

"Now, we have to go into town to get this flat fixed, or we won't have a spare. I'll expect you boys to be on your best behavior, you hear? Don't run off, don't goof off, don't do anything foolish. Just stay in the back of the pickup and be nice."

That's all the bonus I got. A ride into town.

Fine. I could wait. Being nice in town was second nature to me, but I would try to keep a close eye on Drover. Drover was the problem, see. You never knew what the little goof might do next. I would hock him like a watch.

Watch him like a hawk, shall we say.

We set out for town. After driving over three miles of dusty roads, we turned left on the highway and picked up speed. As you might expect, I occupied my place of honor on the spare tire, which was now a flat spare tire, and enjoyed letting the wind blow my ears around. I reached a very peaceful state of . . . well, peacefulness and contentment, and had just about forgotten about the Phony Bonus, when I heard Drover's voice.

"Hank, look who's behind us."

I opened my eyes and saw . . . well, a pickup,

an old blue pickup. "Yes? And so what?"

"Don't you recognize it?"

"No, I . . ." Wait a minute. Hadn't I seen that pickup before? There was something familiar about it. I sat up, narrowed my eyes, and studied it. "Drover, do you see who's behind us? That's Joe McCall."

"Yeah, I know."

"Don't you see what this means? If that's the same pickup, then it's probably got a big, ugly rottweiler in the back."

"Yeah, I know. Bruiser."

"Let's see, what did they call that mutt?"

"Bruiser."

"Ah, yes, Bruiser. And notice, Drover, that he's looking at us from around the cab!"

"Oh my gosh, don't make him mad."

"Relax, son. He's in a moving pickup. He can't touch us. Watch this." I left the spare tire and swaggered toward the back of the pickup. I stuck out my tongue and crossed my eyes.

"Hank, I think he's getting mad. He's making fangs and I think he's barking."

"Good. Great. That's just what he deserves, the big creep. Now watch this." I turned around and showed him my backside. I even moved my hiney back and forth. "What does he think about that?"

"Oh my gosh, he's really mad now. Are you sure he can't jump into our pickup?"

"It's impossible, Drover. We've got him just where we want him."

Joe McCall pulled out into the other lane, stomped on the gas, and passed us. He honked and waved at Slim, and as they went around us, I found myself looking directly into the . . . oooo boy . . . into the hideous, angry, ugly face of Bruiser himself.

I gave him a little grin and a wave. "Hi. How y'all doing? You sure are ugly. I've seen toads with prettier faces than yours. If I was as ugly as you, I'd wear a sack over my head."

They zoomed passed us. Chuckling to myself, I made my way back to the spare tire. Drover was lying flat, with his paws pulled up over his eyes. He was moaning and quivering, and you know what else? He started singing this song. After a moment, I couldn't help but join him. Here, listen.

**It's Not Smart to Show
Your Hiney to a Bear**

Drover
Hank, you're giving me a bad case
    of the shivers,

And this leg is really causing me some pain.
'Cause that dog is mean enough to eat
    our livers.
All that's stopping him is just a piece of chain.

    If he ever took a notion he might break
        the chain in half,
    And I think that I would perish from
        the fright.
    Would you please show some restraint,
    Before I up and faint?
    Just sit down before you get us in a fight.

Hank
Drover, what is the nature of your problem?
So I taunted him and had a little fun.
Heck, he's just a dog and not some
    awful goblin.
If he jumps us, I'll just whip him. You can run.

    See, when you're hanging with the
        Head of Ranch Security,
    You don't need to have a plan or hedge
        your bets.
    Sure, I guess he's kind of large,
    But Drover, I'm in charge,
    So relax, enjoy the ride, and cool your jets.

Drover
Yeah, but Hank, I really wish you
    wouldn't do this.
Making enemies is not a funny joke.
See, I really would prefer that I lived through
    this,
And if he jumped into our pickup, I'd
    just croak.

What goes around will come around,
    I'll bet the day will come
When you'll wish that you'd resisted
    just a hair.
You say, "What the heck,"
But I'm a nervous wreck.
It's not smart to show your hiney to a bear.

When the song was over, I gave the runt a smile.
"Relax, Drover. We'll never see that creep again."
    "Yeah? How can you be so sure?"
    "Because it would be too much of a coincidence.
All the odds are against it. Things like that just
don't happen in the real world."
    And sure enough, we didn't see the big oaf again.
    Until twenty minutes later.

CHAPTER TEN

I Impress All the Lady Dogs in Town

When I heard the pickup slowing down, I sat up and looked out. Sure enough, we were approaching the town of Twitchell.

This was where Slim and Loper came to buy windmill parts and ranch supplies, and where Sally May came to shop for groceries and clothes. It was a huge and exciting place. Hundreds of people lived here, maybe even thousands.

Main Street was long and wide, crawling with cars and people, and it had every kind of store and shop you could imagine: two drugstores, a five-and-dime store, three hardware stores, and several stores that sold clothes and stuff. Oh, and there was even a livestock auction on the north end of town, near the grain elevator.

The grain elevator was the tallest building in town, a big, round white structure that you could see from miles away. It was a building for grain, not people. They used it for storing wheat, don't you see, after it was harvested in the summer.

We dogs didn't get to come to town very often, and for us it was a pretty big deal. It gave us a chance to see new sights, to bark at new dogs, and . . . well, there was always the chance that, while motoring down Main, we might even catch a glimpse of a lady dog or two.

Pretty exciting, huh? You bet it was, and as we made our way down Main Street, I found myself sitting a little higher in the spare tire, holding my head at a prouder angle, and, you know, putting on my best appearance, just in case we saw one. Lady dog, that is.

The lady dogs are very impressed by any dog who rides in the back of a pickup. Maybe you didn't know that, but they are, and the kind of pickup that impresses them most is the very kind we were riding in—a big four-wheel-drive ranch rig with mud flaps on the back, that's pulling a stock trailer.

I don't know what it is about mud flaps, but the women just go nuts over a dog who owns a big four-wheel-drive pickup with mud flaps.

So I was definitely on the alert, and sure enough, when we stopped for a red light in the middle of town, I glanced to my left and saw . . . mercy! She was a golden retriever, sitting up in the front seat of a yellow car.

A green car. Who cares? It was a car.

She was gorgeous. Long flowing ears, deep brown eyes, a shiny coat of hair, and a wonderful long nose. Her window was down halfway and I noticed that she tossed a glance in my direction.

No, it was even better than that. She tossed a glance *at me*, looked away, and then turned her adoring eyes back on me and *stared*. I, uh, wiggled my left eyebrow at her, and, oh, you should have

seen her response! She lifted her ears, ever so slightly, and smiled.

Well, that told me all I needed to know. I heaved myself up from the spare tire, tossed a wink at Drover (he'd been watching the whole thing), and swaggered over to the side of the pickup.

"Howdy, ma'am," I said in my deepest, most malodorous voice. "I don't think I've ever seen you at this stoplight before."

Her response caused my old heart to swell up like . . . something. Red beans soaking in a bowl of water, I suppose. She said, and this is a direct quote, she said, "Oh?"

Wow!

I went on. "Yes ma'am. You see, I own a big ranch south of town. I seldom come to Twitchell, and when I do, I don't get many opportunities to . . . well, chat with the ladies at a stoplight."

And she said—check this out—she said, "Oh?"

Wow!

I had her going, fellers. I could see the light in her eyes and hear the quiver of romance in her voice. I didn't slow down or back up. No sir, I plunged on and went straight to the Big Ticket.

"I noticed you . . . admiring my mud flaps."

Her eyes seemed to . . . well, blank out, I guess you would say. "Your what?"

She was being coy. I had caught her stealing glances at the mud flaps, see, and she didn't want me to know. I guess. With these women, it's hard to tell what's really going on. They give you a sign and pretend they didn't. They say one thing and mean another.

It's kind of confusing, to tell you the truth, but I was pretty sure I had her going in the right direction. I plunged on and showed her a wolfish smile.

"My mud flaps. They're pretty nice, huh? They're heavy duty. Only the biggest and . . ."

Oops. The light changed and we were moving forward. It caught me off guard and I had to do a little scrambling around to keep my balance, but fortunately the lady's car stayed beside our pickup.

I continued, speaking louder to be heard over the roar of the pickup. "Only the biggest and best of your ranch pickups have these heavy-duty mud flaps. The women really seem to like them. And I noticed you . . ." Slim let off the gas and shifted gears, causing me to stagger. "I saw you admiring them."

She shook her head and said—I'll keep these words close to my heart forever and ever—she said, "Leroy, I don't know what you're talking about, but if you don't sit down, you're going to fall out and get yourself smashed all over Main Street."

The car pulled away, leaving me alone with my pounding heart and the glowing memory of her lovely face. My whole body tingled. She had called me . . . *Leroy*. No doubt that was some kind of code word which meant "Lover Boy" or "You Handsome Rascal."

And her concern that I might get "smashed all over Main Street" proved, beyond the shallow of a doubt, that she *really cared*.

Sigh!

I never saw her again, and she never saw me again, but we'd enjoyed our precious moment together. I would keep the memory of it forever in the little cigar box of my heart.

I heaved a sigh and waved a farewell, just as Slim turned a corner and almost threw me out. Did he have to turn corners at thirty miles an hour? With my claws scraping on the bed of the pickup, I fought my way back to the spare tire and collapsed.

Drover was staring at me. "What was that all about?"

"She loves me, Drover. I could see it in her eyes."

"I'll be derned. I thought you were talking about trucks."

"We were talking about love, Drover, but with these women, you don't go straight to the point."

"How come?"

"Because . . . because you don't, that's all. You don't just run up and kiss 'em. You surround 'em, so to speak, with intelligent, witty conversation, and before they know it, they're madly in love."

"I'll be derned. I wish I had a way with the women. I never know what to say."

"Just watch me and study your lessons, son. The next time you encounter a lady dog on the street, start talking about mud flaps. It works every time."

He gave a shrug and returned to the black hole of his thoughts . . . if he had any thoughts. I wasn't sure he did, but at least I had tried to help him out with his problems in the Lady Department. I was always glad to help Drover along Life's Path of . . . something.

Moments later, Slim pulled up in front of Jim's Tire Service. I stood up and was in the middle of a nice Yawn and Stretch, when he slammed on the stupid brakes, throwing me against the cab. He stepped out and saw me . . . well, picking myself up, and he grinned.

"Stand up, pooch. We ain't in the country anymore, so don't embarrass me."

Very funny. He'd slammed on the brakes *on purpose,* knowing perfectly well that it would send us dogs flying around in the back. He did it all the time. It was another of his pathetic attempts at humor. It wasn't funny the first time, and it got unfunnier and unfunnier the more he did it.

Oh well.

The tire shop was located in a big metal building. Slim got the flat tire out of the back of the pickup and rolled it inside. I hopped down and followed a few steps behind. Suddenly my nose began picking up a strange odor. It was strong and it smelled a lot like . . . well, rubber.

Ah yes. This was a tire shop, right? And tires are made of rubber, yes? So there we were. It was all fitting together.

Several men were working inside, changing flats and making a lot of racket. One of them saw us and came toward us. Description: shorter than Slim and stocky in build, khaki pants and shirt, dark hair and eyes, and a nice smile. Oh, and his name was stitched on the front of his shirt: Miguel.

He and Slim seemed to know each other. They shook hands and made small talk. The substance of their conversation, as I recall, was that the weather had been too hot and too dry, and that we needed a rain. I agreed with all that.

Slim pointed to his tire. "I'm broke down, Miguel. Reckon you can fix me up?"

"No problem." He took the tire and laid it up on a rack and started airing it up.

Slim slouched against the wall and glanced around the building. "Where's that dog-eating cat of yours?"

Miguel looked up and grinned. "Pico? He's around. He hides and waits. When a dog comes close . . ." Miguel made claws and growled.

Well, that got my attention. A "dog-eating cat"? I'd never heard of such a thing, and suddenly I found my eyes prowling the racks of tires at the rear of the . . . *there he was!* A big Siamese tomcat. He was perched on top of some tires, staring at me with weird blue eyes. Oh, and he was flicking the tip of his tail.

Our gazes met. Through my eyes, I sent the cat a message: "Pal, I don't know who you are or who you *think* you are, but the last kitty that tried to eat *me* spent some time in the hospital."

The cat—Pico was his name, I suppose— received my eye-message and . . . well, didn't show much response at all, to tell you the truth, which proved that he was just another dumb cat. If he'd had any sense at all, he would have left the building and found a place to hide.

Remember my motto? "Do unto others but don't take trash off the cats." That goes double for cats who have wild fantasies about eating dogs. Dumb cat.

I was in the midst of glaring my message at that fraud of a blue-eyed tomcat, when Miguel's gaze drifted down to me. "That your dog?"

Slim nodded. "Sort of. Me and the boss take turns with him. It's kind of like sharing a cold. One of us has him for a while and passes him on the other."

Miguel chuckled. "He looks like a pretty good dog."

"I guess he's as good as I deserve. He eats too much and he ain't too smart, but people say the same about me."

Miguel put his ear to the tire and listened for a hiss of air. He found the spot and pulled out a nail with a pair of pliers. "Can he burp?"

"Say what?"

"The dog. Can he burp?"

A grin spread across Slim's mouth. "Well I . . . I never thought about that, Miguel. I suppose he can, but I can't say as I've ever studied it real close."

"I could make him burp. Right now, any time, on command."

Slim hitched up his jeans. He was still grinning. "Now wait a minute. You're saying you can tell him to burp and he'll burp?"

Miguel nodded. "I'm a dog trainer. You want to see?"

Some of the other men had gathered around. One of them nodded and said, "Miguel can do it. He trains dogs, all kinds of dogs."

Slim pushed his hat to the back of his head and chewed on his lip. "Well, this I've got to see. I don't think you can do it."

Miguel reached for his wallet. "Five bucks says I can."

"Uh-uh. I ain't a wealthy man like you, Miguel." Slim whipped out his wallet. "But by grabs, I've got a one-dollar bill that says you can't."

"You're covered." Miguel laid a dollar bill on the cement floor and Slim laid one right beside it. "What's the dog's name?"

"Oh, he's got many names, depending on how mad we are at him, but he goes by Hank most of the time."

"I will teach Hank to burp on command." Miguel disappeared into the office.

My gaze and Slim's met. Neither of us had any idea what was coming next.

Oh, and that blue-eyed Siamese cat was watching.

CHAPTER ELEVEN

You'll Never Guess
Who Showed Up

Miguel went into the office and came back with a bowl and a can of . . . something. Soda pop? Yes, it was soda pop. He set the bowl down in front of me and poured the pop into it. Then he stood over me and pointed to the bowl.

"That's for you, Hank. Soda pop, good stuff. Take a drink."

I looked up into his eyes and whapped my tail on the floor. He'd brought a soda pop, just for me? Gee, what a nice guy. I mean, I'd always had a fondness for soda pop, especially on hot summer days, but on our ranch I seldom got any. The cowboys are kind of stingy, don't you know, and . . .

Well, this was very touching. A fresh, cool soda pop, just for ME. I leaned forward and gave

111

it a sniffing. It smelled . . . cool and refreshing. Wonderful. My mouth began to water and I found myself, uh, licking my chops. I rolled my eyes up to Miguel, just to be sure this wasn't a trick.

He nodded and pointed to the bowl. "For you, doggie."

Well . . . okay. I mean, if he was buying the drinks, I sure wasn't going to insult him by turning him down. I started lapping. It was even better and sweeter and refreshinger than I had supposed. Great stuff. I lapped it all down and even licked the bottom . . .

Huh?

In a flash, Miguel reached down, picked me up, and started . . . what was the deal here? He was *shaking me*. He shook me several times, pretty hard, and then set me back down on the cement floor.

"Now, Hank," he said, shooting a grin at Slim, "I command you to burp."

What? Burp? Hey, I couldn't just . . .

"Go on, doggie, let's hear a big one."

Gee, I hated to disappoint him, but who can . . .

All at once I felt a rumbling in my stomach, and something began moving up the stovepipe of my . . .

BORK!

My ears leaped up. Was that . . . me?

The men who had gathered around us broke

into laughter and applause. Miguel beamed a smile, clapped his hands together, and snatched the two dollar bills off the floor. Slim leaned his head back and laughed out loud.

"You cheated, Miguel, but that's okay. It was worth a buck."

Miguel leaned over and patted me on the head.

"Good dog, Hank. You are very smart. Stay away from Pico."

Well, I . . . I hardly knew how to respond. I mean, we ranch dogs aren't used to so much kindness and attention, and heck, if Miguel wanted to bring me another soda pop . . .

Suddenly they were all gone, back to work fixing tires, clanging and banging and making hissing noises, and I found myself all alone. Oh well. One minute a star, the next minute just another dog on the street. But it had been nice, basking in the limejuice and enjoying my brief moments of . . . BUPP . . . excuse me, fame.

They were making so much racket in there, it was hurting my ears, so I headed outside. And let me hasten to add that my leaving the shop had nothing to do with the so-called "dog-eating cat." It had suddenly occurred to me that Drover needed another lecture on . . . something or other. He could always use another lecture, so I . . . it had nothing to do with the cat.

A blue pickup pulled up in front of the shop. A man came inside, rolling a tire. We passed, and I had to get out of his way, otherwise he might have run over me with his tire. I hopped up into the back of Slim's pickup and saw Drover.

What was he doing now? His eyes were wide

open and he seemed to be jerking his head toward . . . my eyes went to the back of the blue pickup, and I found myself staring right into the ugly face of . . .

You'll never guess who it was. Bruno the Boxer? Nope. Rufus the Doberman Pinscher? Nope. Rambo the Great Dane? Wrong again. No, it was the face of a wottreiler, and I happened to know the guy. His name was Bruiser.

Are you shocked? I knew you would be, but the tipoff was the blue pickup, don't you see. I had identified it the very moment . . . okay, maybe I'd missed that little clue, but the important thing was that Bruiser was sitting in a pickup, not ten feet away from us. And he looked MAD. Real mad.

He recognized me. "So, it's you again."

All at once I felt myself . . . uh . . . sinking and shrinking and slinking, shall we say, and wilting under the glare of that big ape. Yipes! Who could look into such terrible eyes? And all at once I began to regret all the . . . uh . . . rude and tacky things I had . . .

"Drover, don't say a word, not one word. We have entered into a situation here that could prove to be very dangerous."

"Yeah, I know."

Bruiser's voice cut through the silence like a

chain saw. "Hey, you. Dummy. Come here."

I shot a glance at Drover. His teeth were chattering. "I think he's speaking to you, Drover."

"Oh my gosh, I knew we'd see him again! I knew you shouldn't have . . . What if he comes over here? What'll we do?"

I cut my eyes from side to side. I had just noticed an important detail. "Drover, do you see what I see? He's chained to the pickup. Look, see for yourself."

"Well, I'll be derned, he is. Chained to the pickup."

"Do you understand the meaning of this?"

"Well, let me think. It means that if we hide and keep quiet, he won't bust the chain and kill us."

I gave him a stern glare. "No. That's not what it means. It means that he's helpless and harmless. It means that he's just another wimpy mutt who couldn't hurt a fly. It means that we can give him more of what he deserves for trying to kill our helpless baby deer."

A goofy grin spread across Drover's mouth. "I'll be derned. I never thought of that. You mean . . ."

"Yes, exactly." I gave him a sly wink. "Do you remember the routine?"

"The same one we used on Bruno the Boxer?"

"That's the one." I gave him a pat on the shoulder. "You go first."

"Well . . . are you sure? It's kind of a small chain."

"Don't worry, Drover. No dog is strong enough to break a chain. Go for it."

He hopped down to the ground and walked around to the side of Bruiser's pickup. He looked up into Bruiser's ugly face. "Oh, hi there. We were just wondering if you'd mind if we wet down your tires."

Bruiser's eyes widened. "Stay away from my tires, you little shrimp, or I'll wring your neck."

Drover swallowed hard. "Yeah, but you're on a chain, and Hank says you can't break it."

"Hank's brain can't keep up with his mouth."

Drover glanced at me and giggled. "Yeah, but I think we'll mark your tires and see what happens."

Drover took the left side and I took the right. We slapped a good strong mark on all four tires. Just as I had suspected, the cowardly rottweiler growled and grumbled, but he didn't lunge against the chain. Even as dumb as he was, he knew he couldn't break it.

We regrouped near the door on the driver's side. "Nice work, Drover. I don't know as I've ever seen you do a better job of marking tires."

He grinned and wiggled his stub tail. "Yeah, it was fun. You reckon we ought to give 'em a second coat?"

He glanced up at Bruiser. So did I. What we saw shocked us both.

See, you probably thought Bruiser would be near-crazy with anger, right? Furious and ready to tear us apart? Well, he wasn't. What we saw were . . . tears shining in the corners of his eyes. Honest. I'm not kidding.

Drover and I exchanged puzzled glances. This was NOT what we had expected.

Then Bruiser spoke. "You guys are right. I'm just a big, ugly lunk. I'm a bad dog, I've always been a bad dog, and everybody hates me. But you know what, fellas? Inside this huge, ugly body, there's a little scottie terrier who wants just one thing in the world." He looked up to the sky. "*A friend!*"

Again, Drover and I exchanged glances. I could see that Drover's lower lip was beginning to tremble. And heck, maybe mine was too. I mean, this was kind of . . . touching.

He went on. "You hate me, I know you do, and I'm glad you hate me. I deserve it. But . . ." He glanced away and bit his lower lip. ". . . then there's the story nobody ever hears about old Bruiser. I was orphaned as a pup and raised by junkyard dogs. Every morning and every evening, they . . . beat me."

Drover's mouth was hanging open. "They beat you? Why, that's terrible!"

Big tears slid down his big, ugly face. "Yes, they beat me and made me mean. Over and over they said to me, they said, 'Bruiser, you're no good. You're nothing but a rotten rottweiler.' And you know what, fellas? After a guy hears that over and over, day after day, he begins to . . ."

He couldn't finish. He broke down and started crying—sobbing. I found myself looking at Drover. "What have we done?"

Drover was beginning to cry. "I don't know, but I feel awful!"

"Yeah, me too. What a louse I've turned out to be! I told the poor guy that he walked like a fat duck."

"Yeah, and you showed him your hiney."

"Yes, and I regret that now."

"I'm sorry I wet on his tires and I wish I could take it all back."

"I know, but it's too late, Drover. It's water under the tire." I heaved a sigh. "Well, there's only one thing left to do."

"What? Tell me. I'm ready to do anything."

"Let's jump up into the back of his pickup and grant him his fondish wist: *we'll become his friends.* We'll convince him that he's not just a rotten dog, that's he's really a wonderful fellow."

Drover was staring at me. "You mean . . . you know, I don't think that's such a great idea."

119

"Hey, you said you were ready to do anything. If we surround this guy with warmth and friendship, Drover, it could change his whole life. What's more, it would make us feel better, knowing that we had befriended such a miserable wretch."

"Yeah, but you know this old leg of mine. It's giving me fits and I don't think I could make the jump."

"Okay, fine, have it your own way. You'll be sorry, of course. I'll get all the credit for turning his life around, and you, Drover, you'll have to live with the fact that you marked the tires of a helpless, broken dog."

"I only marked two of 'em."

"Yes, two tires, Drover, and that was just enough to break his heart. I hope you're happy."

"It works for me."

"What?"

"I said, I hope I can live with the guilt."

I marched around to the back of the pickup and prepared to begin my Errand of Mercy, salvaging what was left of poor Bruiser's life and self-esteemer.

I hardly noticed that Drover had scrambled under Slim's pickup. Or that Pico was still watching.

CHAPTER TWELVE

My Triumph over the Raging Rottweiler

With a heavy heart, I hopped up into the back of Bruiser's pickup. The poor guy was curled up in a ball near the front—all alone, unwanted, abandoned, hated by everyone. I went to him and laid a paw on his shoulder.

"I've come to help, Bruiser. Go on with your story."

He raised up, and through teary eyes, he said, "Gosh, you really want to hear it?"

"Yes. I think it's important that you tell it all to . . . *a friend.*"

"You'd . . . you'd consider being my friend?"

I lifted my eyes toward heaven and nodded. "Yes. You see, Bruiser, those of us in the Security

Business appear to be tough and hard. That's only because our job demands it. But peel off the outer layers of steel and iron, and you find dogs who really care."

"Oh gosh!"

"So let it all spill out. I'm here not to judge but to listen."

"Well, okay." He wiped a tear from his eye. "Those mugs in the junkyard, they made me mean, see, and they told me I was rotten and nasty to the core."

"Hmmm, this is so sad."

"Yeah, but then one day I had this . . . this kind of revelation, you might say, and I looked back on my terrible wasted life . . . and I realized . . . *they were right.*"

HUH?

"What did you just say?"

"I said," he rose to his feet, "they were right about me. I was rotten to the core, and that's just the way I wanted it."

He seemed to be . . . there was a strange light in his eyes, see, and . . . gulp.

"Hey, wait a minute. You said that deep inside your inner bean, you're actually a . . . uh . . . little scottish terrier. That's exactly what you said. Honest. I heard it."

"Heh, heh. One of the things that makes me so rotten, pal, is that I lie all the time. I love telling lies to saps like you who believe anything. And you know what else I love?"

"Uh . . . your fellow dogs?"

"Naaa. I love getting revenge."

I began backing away. "Revenge? But you're chained up. Don't forget that."

"Ha, ha. Watch this." He took one step backward and lunged against the chain. It snapped.

I stared at the two ends of the chain. I swallowed hard. All at once my mouth seemed . . . uh . . . very dry. *Gack! Bruiser was loose and I was standing in the back of his pickup!*

"Bruiser, let me speak frankly. I feel that I've been tricked and used."

A jagged laugh erupted from his throat. "Oh yeah? Well, you ain't been used like you're fixing to be used, 'cause I'm fixing to use you for a mop."

"A mop? Now wait . . ." I began creeping backward. He crept toward me. "I thought you wanted a friend."

"Yeah, I lied. What would a guy like me do with a friend? Huh? I'd just beat him up. That's me, pal. Rotten to the core."

"But I thought . . . wait, stop. I have one more thing to say. It's very important."

He gave me a smirk. "Yeah? What?"

I turned my gaze to the sky and heaved a heavy sigh. "Bruiser . . . good-bye!"

ZOOM!

He had given me just enough time to get the heck out of there. I hit Full Turbos, went flying off the bed of the pickup, and set a speed course for the inside of Jim's Tire Shop.

"Here he comes, Drover, get him!"

Drover did nothing, of course. As I roared past Slim's pickup, I saw the little mutt quivering underneath, with his paws over his eyes. It was a short glimpse, because I was hauling the mail for safer ground.

See, I had realized that this was no normal dog. He had a loose screw somewhere in his head, and he seemed pretty determined to . . . well, tear me to shreds.

I, on the other hand, was just as determined not to be torn to shreds, and I had some hope that the guys inside might come to my rescue. I mean, Slim was a great pal of mine, and Miguel . . . remember Miguel? We were the best of buds, had shared many laughs and good times, and don't forget that I had burped for him only minutes before.

I went flying into the shop, with Bruiser right

on my tail, snarling and slashing the air with his bear-trap jaws. The men heard us coming. They stopped their work and turned their eyes to the riot in progress.

Joe McCall saw what was happening. He was sitting in a chair and leaped to his feet. Miguel grabbed a tire tool. Slim just stood there, too surprised to move.

Joe made a dive for Bruiser. "Here, Bruiser, easy boy, nice doggie." He managed to grab a hind leg, but that dog was so big and strong, he broke away.

Then Bruiser turned his eyes back to me and charged! I ran to the far end of the shop, hoping . . . the back door was shut! My eyes darted around the shop. There was only one way out, and Bruiser stood between me and the outside world.

I stood there, frozen, petrified. Bruiser grinned and started toward me again. "Now, where were we?"

"We were . . . listen, Bruiser, if you're torqued about all those things I said about you, I think I can explain everything. Honest."

"Yeah? Give it a try."

"Great. Okay, I said you were ugly, right? Not true, not true at all. You're actually a very handsome guy."

He laughed and advanced another step toward me. "I'm ugly."

I edged backward and bumped against the wall. "Okay, you're ugly. We're straight on that one. I said you walk like a fat duck, remember? Ha, ha. What a wild exaggeration! I don't know what came over me to make such a . . ."

"What about chasing fawns?"

"Chasing fawns?"

"Yeah. Is that right or wrong? See, yesterday you hurt my feelings. You made me feel bad for chasing a baby deer."

"Yes, I suppose I did."

"So take it back. Tell me it's okay if I want to chase a baby deer the next time I visit your ranch. Say it and I'll let you walk out of here alive."

I took a big gulp of air. All at once I wasn't scared anymore. "Bruiser, you've just reminded me how much I disliked you the first time we met. I mean, when I saw you jump on that poor little deer, I felt nothing but disgust, and it's all coming back to me now. You're not only big and ugly and stupid, but you're disgusting. And you know what, Bruiser? I'm fixing to give you the whipping you've needed for a long time."

A nasty laugh poured out of his throat. "You're

crazy, cowdog." He took a step backward. "I'm twice as big as you are."

I raised the hair on my back and advanced. "Yep, and that gives me twice the target and twice as much fun. Stand your ground, son. Here come the marines."

His eyes flicked from side to side. He took another step backward. "I'll hurt you, I'll hurt you bad."

"That's okay. The vet clinic's just down the road. Let's get it over with."

He took another step backward. Was he retreating or setting me up for something? I couldn't tell and it didn't matter. I coiled my legs like steel springs and jumped into the middle of him, and then . . . a great rolling darkness moved over me, and that was the last thing I remembered.

You're probably wondering what happened. Did I manage to survive or did that monster of a dog tear off my legs and ears and leave me for dead?

Well, let's mush on and see.

I awoke on the floor. I had no feeling in my legs or tail, and all the early indicators suggested that . . . you'd better hold on to something . . . it appeared that my neck had been broken and that I would be paralyzed for life.

Bruiser had threatened to "wring" my neck,

remember? Well, the early reports from Data Control suggested that if he hadn't actually wrung my neck, he had come pretty close.

I saw a circle of faces above me. I recognized Slim's right away. He looked pale and very concerned. And there was Joe. I remembered Joe, a nice guy who kept a bad dog. Oh, and there was Miguel, my old burping partner. It was good to see him again, only he sure looked worried about something.

ME, no doubt. Yes, I was in bad shape, very serious condition. Nobody needed to tell me I was critically wounded. I could see it in their faces. I hated being such a burden to them, and to show the depth of my concern, I whapped my . . .

I whapped my tail on the cement floor, and that was odd. I mean, if a guy's paralyzed . . .

Slim spoke. "Boys, I don't see a single mark on him. You don't reckon he just . . . fainted, do you?"

Fainted! Ha! What kind of crazy talk was that? It was perfectly clear what had happened. I had gone into combat against one of the biggest, meanest, heartlessest rottweiler dogs in the whole Texas Panhandle, and though I had fought a brave fight, Bruiser had inflicted enormous, inclackulable damage upon my body.

No, I had *not* fainted. I just happened to have

a *broken neck,* and maybe we should start thinking about rushing me to the vet clinic, huh? Would that be too much trouble?

At that moment, Drover came padding up. He looked down at me and grinned.

Since I couldn't move my head, not with all the shattered and splintered neck bones, I rolled my eyes around so that I could see him. "What are you grinning about?"

"Oh, that was quite a fight. Never saw anything like it."

"Pretty bad, I guess. Did I land any punches?"

"Nope, not a one."

"I was afraid of that. Well, I did my best, Drover, and now you'll have to carry on without me."

"No, just when the fight was about to start, this big blue-eyed tomcat came out of nowhere and jumped on top of Bruiser's head. Boy, what a show! Old Bruiser ran like a striped ape and jumped up in the back of Joe's pickup. Remember? He's scared of cats."

HUH?

I rose to my feet and stuck my nose in the runt's face. "Hey, don't tell me there wasn't a fight. I was there, pal, I was in the middle of it. It was one of the most ferocious combat experiences of my entire . . ."

I blinked my eyes and looked around. The men were all smiling, and all at once they . . . well, were clapping their hands . . . applauding . . . and I suddenly realized . . .

What we had here was a sudden reversal, you might say, and although I had been badly wounded in combat, the bones in my neck had miraculously . . . okay, maybe I'd fainted, but who wouldn't have fainted?

What matters is that I won. And Miguel's cat had nothing to do with it.

So it all worked out pretty well. The last I saw of Bruiser, he was sitting in the back of Joe's pickup, sniffling about his unhappy childhood and promising to be a good dog for the rest of his life.

Pretty neat, huh? Against incredible odds, I had wrapped up the Case of the Raging Rottweiler and had even helped Bruiser find his true creampuff self. Things had turned out so well, I even removed the six Chicken Marks from Drover's record.

Just another day in the life of a cowdog.

Case closed.

Okay, maybe the cat helped a little bit, but not much, so don't be spreading lies about how I was . . .

Skip it.

What does the future hold for the Head of Ranch Security?

I n his next adventure, Hank the Cowdog enters into a battle of wits with Pete the Barncat, goes in search of the golden pot of chicken at the end of the rainbow, and challenges Rip and Snort to the Deadly Ha-Ha Game. Will he survive it all with his usual good humor? Turn the page to find out what's in store for Hank in *Hank the Cowdog #37: The Case of the Deadly Ha-Ha Game.*

In Search
of a Treasure

When Loper and Little Alfred went inside the house, I made my way down the hill and to the Security Division's vast office complex. I punched in the entry code on the door and took the elevator up to the . . . okay, we didn't have an elevator, and our "office complex" consisted of a couple of ragged gunnysacks beneath the gas tanks.

Might as well admit the truth.

It was a shabby place to house the entire Security Division, but that was the kind of cheapjohn outfit I worked for. You'd think the cowboys would have . . . skip it. We don't want to get started on that subject.

Anyway, I took the elevator up to the twelfth floor and entered the office, glanced at a stack of

1

reports on my desk and checked for messages. An odd sound reached my ears, and it was then that I noticed Drover. He had crawled beneath his gunnysack and appeared to be . . . moaning.

I flopped down in my chair. "Okay, Drover, out with it. What's the problem?"

One corner of his gunnysack rose and I saw one big round eye peeking out. "What makes you think I've got a problem?"

"Because you're hiding under your bed."

"Oh, you noticed."

"Of course I noticed. And furthermore, I happen to know that when you hide under your bed, you're usually fleeing from Reality as It Really Is. So, out with it, let's get it over with."

He poked his nose out. "Well, okay. I have a broken heart."

"Broken heart. Go on. What seems to be the problem?"

"Well, I got caught with the steak and Little Alfred thought I stole it, and he . . . he called me a naughty dog!" With that, he broke into tears and boo-hoos. "It just breaks my heart!"

I gave the runt a moment to get control of himself. "Well, what can I say? You had the steak in your mouth and you got caught. You're old enough to start accepting the consequences of your own actions."

"Yeah, but it was *your* action. You stole the steak and I was just ..."

"Hold it, stop right there, halt. I've already spotted a hole in your ointment. You said I stole the steak."

"Yeah, 'cause you did. I saw it myself."

"Drover, I didn't steal the steak. I had merely gathered evidence for an investigation, and that evidence just happened to be a steak."

"Yeah, but you were going to eat it. And when I saw that you were about to eat it, I wanted to eat it too, and I just couldn't control myself, and ..." He broke down crying again. "And I got caught and now I'm a naughty dog!"

This was very sad, but I tried to hide my emotions. "I guess there's an important lesson here, son. When we fail to control our lower impulses, we get ourselves into trouble. Haven't I warned you about that? We must learn to say no to the voice of temptation."

"Yeah, but you stole the steak off the plate and I got blamed! It's not fair! All my life, I've wanted to be a good dog."

"I know you have, but Drover, you must face the fact that life is often unfair. The important thing here is that life was unfair to *you*, thus sparing me a lot of shame and embarrassment.

Isn't that worth something? I mean, think about my position on this ranch. How would it look if the Head of Ranch Security got nailed for stealing a steak?"

He wiped a tear out of his eye. "Well, it would look like the truth."

"Exactly, and the truth is very important, but there are different shades of truth. The very best kind of truth is the kind that doesn't cast dark shadows on the reputations of our leaders. It was very brave of you to defend the right kind of truth."

"It was? You really think so?"

"Oh yes, no question about it. Very brave. And I wouldn't be surprised if this brought you a little promotion."

His face burst into a smile and he crawled out from under his bed. "No fooling? A promotion for me?"

"Yes sir, a nice little promotion for bravery in the face of truth."

"Oh goodie! I wonder what it might be."

I studied the claws on my right front foot. "All these years you've held the title of First Assistant Deputy Assistant, right?"

"Gosh, I didn't even know I had a title."

"You did, but now with this act of heroism in your file, we just might bump you up to the next level. How would you like to be . . . First *and* Second Assistant Deputy Assistant?"

"Really? No fooling? Gosh, I'm so proud!"

"Congratulations, soldier, you earned it."

He was hopping for joy, the little . . . He was hopping around and being joyful. "Oh, I'm so happy! Maybe life's not as unfair as I thought."

"Yes, Drover, and behind every silver lining, there's a golden pot."

"Yeah, and every pot has a chicken in it."

"Right. And every chicken must cross the road."

His smile faded. "I wonder why."

"What?"

"Why does a chicken cross the road?"

I chuckled. "That's obvious, isn't it?"

"Not to me."

I began pacing. "Well, a chicken crosses the road . . . When a chicken takes it upon himself to cross a road or trail . . . Drover, I'm afraid we're out of time."

"Oh drat."

"And please try to control your naughty language. Don't forget your new position."

"Oh smurkle."

"That's better." I paused and glanced up at the dark clouds. "What was the point of this conversation?"

5

"Alfred called me a naughty dog and it broke my heart."

"Right, and we cleared that up. You're happy now and you're going to stop drawing me into these ridiculous conversations. I'm a very busy dog and I don't have time to speculate on why chickens cross roads."

"Well, you don't need to get mad."

"I'm not mad. But Drover, I came down here with something important in mind. Now I don't remember what it was. Furthermore, it has suddenly occurred to me that this entire conversation has been . . . loony. Meaningless. This has happened before, Drover, and it troubles me that we continue to carry on loony conversations. Does that bother you?"

He grinned. "No, I kind of enjoy it."

"You enjoy being a loon?"

"Oh, you're never alone when you're with somebody else. It's almost like having company."

"What?"

"I said . . . let me think here. I said, being alone's almost like owning a company, but you have to pay interest on a loan."

Seconds passed as I stared into his eyes. "Oh. Yes, of course." I paced away and tried to shake the vapors out of my head. I still couldn't remember . . .

At that very moment, Drover leaped to his feet and pointed off to the northwest. "Oh look, there's a pretty rainbow. Let's go look for the pot of chicken."

That was it! The rainbow. I had gotten so involved in Drover's personal tragedy that I had forgotten all about Pete's slip of the tongue. "Wait a minute, that was my idea. During my interrogation of the cat, he . . . Wait a minute. What was that you just said about the pot of chicken?"

"Well, let's see here." He rolled his eyes and chewed his lip. "At the end of every rainbow, there's a pot. A pot of chicken."

"Hmmm. I'd always heard that it was a pot of . . . something. Gold."

"No, I think it's chicken. Who'd want to eat gold?"

"Good point. I hadn't thought of that. Maybe it's a golden pot that contains a boiled chicken. That would explain the business about the gold, wouldn't it? Yes, of course. The pieces of the puzzle are falling into place." I glanced over both shoulders and lowered my voice. "Soldier, let's go get that treasure, but don't forget, it was my idea."

With that, we launched ourselves into the evening breeze and went streaking out to claim our rightful share of the Potted Chicken. All at once, Drover's loony conversation became a distant

7

memory, and once again I found myself unmurshed in meaningful work—solving the Case of the Fabled Potted Chicken. *Immersed*, let us say.

With the damp wind blowing in my face, I felt whole again—sane, restored, invigorated. Suddenly I remembered why I had gone into Security Work, and why I would never allow myself to be drawn into another conversation with my lunatic assistant.

Anyway, I was in my element now, back on the job, charging out into the growing darkness to do brave and noble things—and to seize the Fabled Treasure of the Potted Chicken. You've heard of it, I'm sure, the Fabled Treasure of the Potted Chicken. Legends of the ancient Malarkeys and Babushkas had told of a fabulous treasure, don't you see, which could be found at the west end of a rainbow.

Why the west end? Nobody knew the answer to that, but for centuries dogs in America and England and Harmonica and other distant lands had searched in vain for the elusive treasure—a fat boiled chicken in a pot of purest gold. Over the years, thousands of dogs had lost their lives searching for the treasure, and now, by sheer chance and luck, it had come within the grisp of our grasp.

On and on we charged. We could see it up ahead, a big beautiful rainbow, and the west end of it had come to rest right in the middle of our horse pasture!

"There it is, Drover, straight ahead! Now all we have to do is claim it and eat the chicken."

"What about the pot?"

"If we're still hungry after the chicken, maybe we'll eat the pot."

"I'm getting tired, and my leg's killing me."

"Courage, Drover. Just a little farther. You can do it. Gut it out and make it hurt."

"It does."

"Great. Pain is our fuel, son, it's the secret elixative that drives us in this crazy business. We live on pain, we thrive on pain, we . . ."

Huh?

We had reached the middle of the horse pasture, the very spot where the treasure was supposed to be. And there we found . . . sagebrush?

I cut my eyes from side to side. "Drover, something very strange is going on here."

"Yeah," he whispered, "there's two coyotes standing right over there, and they look hungry."

HUH?

You'll never guess . . . I'm sorry, but we'll have to skip this next part.

Too scary.

Have you read all
of Hank's adventures?

Join Hank the Cowdog's Security Force

Are you a big Hank the Cowdog fan? Then you'll want to join Hank's Security Force. Here is some of the neat stuff you will receive:

Welcome Package
- A Hank paperback of your choice
- Free Hank bookmarks

Eight issues of *The Hank Times* with
- Stories about Hank and his friends
- Lots of great games and puzzles
- Special previews of future books
- Fun contests

More Security Force Benefits
- Special discounts on Hank books and audiotapes
- An original Hank poster (19" x 25") absolutely free
- Unlimited access to Hank's Security Force website at www.hankthecowdog.com

Total value of the Welcome Package and *The Hank Times* is $23.95. However, your two-year membership is **only $8.95** plus $3.00 for shipping and handling.

☐ Yes, I want to join Hank's Security Force. Enclosed is $11.95 ($8.95 + $3.00 for shipping and handling) for my **two-year membership**. [Make check payable to Maverick Books.]

Which book would you like to receive in your Welcome Package? Choose any book in the series.

(#   )   (#   )

FIRST CHOICE   SECOND CHOICE

_____

                                        BOY or GIRL
YOUR NAME   (CIRCLE ONE)

_____

MAILING ADDRESS

_____

CITY   STATE   ZIP

_____

TELEPHONE   BIRTH DATE

_____

E-MAIL

Are you a ☐ Teacher or ☐ Librarian?

Send check or money order for $11.95 to:

Hank's Security Force
Maverick Books
P.O. Box 549
Perryton, Texas 79070

DO NOT SEND CASH. NO CREDIT CARDS ACCEPTED.
Allow 4–6 weeks for delivery.

The Hank the Cowdog Security Force, the Welcome Package, and The Hank Times _are the sole responsibility of Maverick Books. They are not organized, sponsored, or endorsed by Penguin Putnam Inc., Puffin Books, Viking Children's Books, or their subsidiaries or affiliates._